The Burden of Joy

Lexi Kent-Monning

Rejection Letters

www.Rejection-Letters.com

ISBN 9798218263454

This is a work of fiction.

Editor: D.T. Robbins
Editorial intern: Bryce Woodcock
Cover design: D.T. Robbins
Cover photo: Lexi Kent-Monning
Author photo: Ruganzu Howard

ONE

New Years

My sinuses can still feel when my ex-husband has had a bad night's sleep. The pressure pounding through my face wakes me up before dawn, and I know he's awake, wherever he is. An owl hoots above, from the flat ledge that five sister cypress trees create. The hooting reverberates around my skull, chasing at a memory that is tickling me, and I realize this owl woke me up last night.

"Is it you?" I now remember gasping, my eyes frantically scanning the other, empty side of my bed, where Daniel used to sleep.

The last few months rush into my consciousness. On the autumn equinox, he had signed up to see a shaman at his new job at the commune. She eyed him as he was surrounded by his new friends who were salivating for her words and, always, for more of Daniel.

"Come back at 9pm," she told him, after several minutes. Once she'd felt his presence, she had to see him after dark. "You are an owl in the night," she announced when he returned.

When Daniel had come home that night, I laid awake and heard two owls. *It's us,* I thought.

On New Year's Eve, our dog Ladybird became entranced by a scent at the base of a pine tree as I walked her. I stood, listless, distracted, cracking my neck. There hadn't been rain for months, and a smear of frosting remained ground down into the street's pavement from a fallen 4th of July cupcake. After toeing at it, I looked up and one foot away from my face, a baby owl sat on a branch. It took me several seconds to register the face staring into mine—its eyes were alien, almost reptilian, and glowing such a fiery orange that I didn't even see the feathers surrounding them at first. *It's our baby*, I thought. *I'll conceive. Our baby will have talons and feathers and golden eyes. It will mind the night, like its father.*

I came home and adorned myself in a sparkling kiss of a dress, smudged dark kohl around my eyes, and drove south along the cliffs hugging the Pacific Ocean towards Big Sur, to Daniel, as the sun set. *We'll be owls in the night as we count to midnight.* We had planned to meet at the top of the commune where Daniel worked, so we could walk down the hill together, which descends quickly into complete darkness. I waited, my eyes adjusting to the night and beginning to see constellations in the sky. The ocean transformed from a vision to a sound and now I could hear the waves tumbling against the cliffs below without seeing them. The music from the commune's New Year party carried up the hill, but not enough to recognize any songs, just the sounds of revelry.

The minutes passed, getting closer to midnight, with no sign of Daniel. This wasn't uncommon, and I tried to shake off my frustration. I touched up my coral lipstick in the rearview mirror with the dome light on, grabbed a flashlight from the car trunk, wrapped my coat around my dress, and walked down the hill alone, the air becoming saltier the longer I walked.

Daniel's office, the guest reservation desk/gift shop, had its lights turned off and door locked. I knocked, waiting to see if he was in the back and stomped my feet to warm up as I waited. Underneath my feet were the action figures Daniel had impishly stuck in the newly poured concrete, which looked like they were drowning now that it had dried. The party was spilling into the patio from the dining hall, which had sustained a few small attempts at decorations, but still resembled a cafeteria. Someone was poking at the toaster with a stick, the sharp scent of charred bread pouring from its top.

Since the summer, I pushed away a subconscious thought I'd had a few times: that I no longer recognized Daniel when I was trying to find him in public. His appearance had changed as drastically as his personality since he began working there less than a year ago. Now I had to remember to look for a man about thirty pounds lighter, wearing clothes that leaned more Hare Krishna than Joe Strummer. I scanned the dining hall again remembering who I had to look for now, rounded the corner, and headed towards the de facto bar.

And that's where I found Daniel, his body wrapped around a woman I had never seen before, but who looked more at home with him than I ever had in our twelve years together. Fight or flight wasn't

summoned. My body inclined towards a quieter response. A child drew in a coloring book on the coffee
table in front of me. Next to him sat a glass of wine
with magic mushrooms floating at the top. My eyes
darted around the room, refusing more information,
before they finally settled reluctantly, shamefully, on
an owl feather hanging from a suede rope. *Is it you?*

Daniel disentangled himself from her when he
saw me. The joy drained from his face and he pushed
the woman's lower back to create a space between
them, to disconnect their touch, but he did it so gently it was a display of intimacy. She drifted reluctantly away from him and towards the abandoned wine
glass. Daniel hugged me like an acquaintance, pat-
ting my back, and when he pulled away, I could see
he had the expression on his face that he made when
he lied.

"Where were you?" I stuttered softly. "I waited at
the top of the hill."

"You found me," he responded, and it sounded
so jovial that even though he had on his lying face,
I believed his show of joy when he gave me a champagne glass and a wink.

Daniel spent the rest of New Year's Eve posturing
as though nothing had happened, but he was over-
compensating: he took photos of me; ran his fingers
up my thighs as we floated in the hot springs, trying
to have sex with me in front of dozens of his coworkers and strangers; and introduced me with a bravado
I'd never seen before, announcing loudly I was his

wife. I remained shell-shocked, mute, and forced a docile smile. The current of shock carried my body through the night, and alcohol blurred my brain enough to carry the rest of me. I was in such a familiar place, with the most familiar person, but I didn't recognize anything.

Finally, we went to a room for staff housing that Daniel and a few others swapped throughout the work week. The person staying before us left the room in filth, crumbs and food stains all over the bed sheets. The mattress was decrepit and alternately swallowed me and punched me with its springs throughout the night. Daniel was exhausted by the evening's events, his frustration at my presence showing now that we were alone.

"My stomach feels like shit. So does my head. Too much champagne," he said as he headed towards the shower. "I just want to go to sleep."

"We have to at least count down to midnight first."

He glanced at his watch as he took it off. "It's 12:03."

Homecoming

I ran out to Daniel's car in the rain, excited and anxious to get my hands on him after three days apart with almost no contact but for a clipped phone call when he'd told me the roads were closed and he was stuck at the commune for a while. I'd let myself ignore the events of the New Year's party and we hadn't spoken of it. I just wanted to try, once more, to keep moving. As I reached his car and saw him moving bags around in his trunk, I could feel a shield surrounding his body.

"I have to talk to you," he nodded at me as he slammed the trunk. He brushed past my arms, which had been wide open to envelop him.

"I'm just not feeling connected here. This cabin doesn't feel right. It kind of makes me feel like a piece of shit," he said, like it was a revelation.

After this abstract proclamation, he again stayed at work for a few days while the roads closed—because of landslides, or because of luck. When he came back, he packed another bag. Each time, more of his things went along with him. I knew what I'd seen on New Year's, but I was still surprised when he stopped coming home.

"We should probably talk to some lawyers and get some paperwork started." This was how I learned Daniel was leaving for good. I'd been stirring lentil soup on the stove and I stared at him, stunned, with the giant wooden spoon suspended in my hand above the soup pot. The spoon was stained yellow from the turmeric in the broth. I ripped his folded arms apart, forced them around me, clawed at his chest, begged him. I didn't beg for anything specific—I didn't have enough information to know what questions to ask. He stood stiff and straight, his hands obligatorily placed on my hips for the first few minutes, until he dropped them to his sides. "Please, please," I pleaded into his chest.

Standing in the kitchen in his unyielding arms, my mind conjured a memory: fourteen years earlier, in the ICU of the hospital in the woods, where my friend was lying with a traumatic brain injury, a punctured lung, a destroyed ear, and other injuries I now can't remember, from a car accident. I held vigil in the waiting room, or in a small corner of his room, or at the nursing station, where I dropped off chocolates and fancy teas to endear our group to the staff. A Brazilian woman was living there while her husband died there. We took turns getting each other coffee and reminded each other to walk a lap or two around the hospital wing. Her husband had fallen unconscious a week ago, out of nowhere, during dinner. He had a brain tumor they hadn't known about and hadn't been awake since. His head had been shaved medically, without a thought of how much it would alter his appearance to his loved ones. His brown skin was pale, and under the blue and green lights of the ICU, looked non-human. Tubes were doing everything for him. And yet his wife gazed at him with such connection and adoration, it was palpable. I never stood where I might obstruct her view of him.

"I believe he'll wake up," she told me in her beautiful accent. She smiled as she said it. "I believe he'll come back to me." In equal parts, I believed it and knew it wasn't true.

When Daniel left, my dreams turned violent: I screamed at the woman from New Year's and smashed beer bottles at her feet, but she didn't see or hear me; a tiger lurked around a pedestrian mall, tame and docile to everyone until it crossed my path, and while I sprinted away frantically, nobody noticed it was lunging after me; a man in a black suit shattered the windows in my living room. After each one I woke up to throbbing sinuses.

Even when I wasn't dreaming, everything seemed to turn to violence. A snarled mess of the formerly living washed up on the beach. The ocean ejected it, farther and farther, towards land. Ladybird rolled in it giddily, and no matter how many times I bathed her, she still reeked of its tangled corpse. It later revealed itself as a wild boar in my photos. What was unidentifiable in person could be seen on film: a hoof, rubbery skin, spare and wiry fur. Daniel and I had thought about having a pig roast at our wedding, but too many of our friends were vegan to have warranted the volume of meat.

Cabin in the Woods

The Carmel Highlands cabin Daniel and I had moved into belonged to my godmother-type-person, Tasha. Atheists don't have godmothers, but if we did, she would be mine. She grew up in the cabin with her parents, Ephraim the artist and Rosa the educator. The Doner house became famous: anyone could drop by at any time, and they would be handed a glass of something to sip by the fireplace, while Rosa and Ephraim began their dance of making dinner together.

Ephraim's studio was in the basement below the house, where he hand painted ceramic tiles and eventually covered the majority of the house's interior with them. The cabin has mostly walls of windows, which peer out to the enormous oak tree, around which the roof has been cut, and a baby redwood tree that is 65 years old, which Tasha calls "little sister." I grew up coming to this cabin, to visit Tasha, to eat a famous Doner meal made by her parents. Then, one day, when Daniel and I were living in LA, Tasha called to say it was ours if we wanted it. We'd wanted it for years, peeked sideways at it whenever we visited Tasha, who moved next door after her parents had died.

During Rosa and Ephraim's time, one of their frequent visitors was Henry Miller, who they'd met in Paris. Henry moved out to Big Sur and became a staple at the Doner house, enamored of Tasha's 5-year-old perspective on his habitual womanizing. He adored her so much, he wrote about her in "Big Sur and the Oranges of Hieronymus Bosch," proclaiming her a "little genius." There are photos of him sitting with each of them at the fireplace, his bright, bald head a shock of white against the fireplace bricks. He spent so much time at the Doner cabin that he eventually had his fourth wedding—though not his last—on the front patio.

Daniel and I had our wedding at the Henry Miller Memorial Library in Big Sur, under the redwood trees, in the thick of the marine layer. Tasha cooked the food for our 100 guests. We would tell people, "We got married at Henry's place, and he got married at ours." Now I can say my first wedding, though maybe not my last, was at Henry's.

When Daniel stopped coming home, I built a fire only a few times, because this fireplace was for us. I couldn't fall asleep without chemicals. I drank gallons of wine. I ate single tablespoons of peanut butter to survive when I knew it had been too long since I'd eaten. I watched hours of death and dismemberment on screens. I gasped for breath, the ocean air never quite filling my lungs. I walked countless miles. I fed Ladybird bowls and bowls of food and water. I begged for a different life as I stared up at tree tops. I stopped writing to-do lists. I started talking with birds. Three times a spider descended onto me from the ceiling, and each time I sighed and lazily removed them from my breast. I stopped locking the doors. I collected feathers. I lost my giggle. I couldn't remember the last time Daniel asked me a question.

In my panic, I bleached my hair. Bleach is cleansing, it can disinfect impurities. I couldn't drink it or douse it on my skin without consequences, but I could coat my hair with it. Every morning that I woke up blonde, I didn't recognize my own hair on my pillow. Its texture completely changed and it didn't feel, smell, or look like mine. It's what I wanted, but it added to my instant feelings of being unnerved every time I woke up. Each day began in a panicked internal monologue: *I'm alone. That's right, because Daniel left. I'm cold. That's right, because my body has started to disappear since he stopped sleeping here. I'm blonde. That's right, because I needed to pour chemicals somewhere to cleanse this suddenly impure life. I'm nauseous. That's right, because my only calories are alcohol.* My natural hair color, red, had begun to feel like a lie. I didn't have an ounce of fire in these bones anymore, not vitality or vim or vigor. Redheads need more anesthesia than blondes or brunettes, but I know I would submit easily, gratefully, to the medically induced sleep.

"I'm not in love with you," Daniel announced into our dark bedroom when he spent one single perfunctory night at home. It was almost a relief to hear him say it. After so many years of taking care of him, wondering and worrying, quelling my instincts, being too tired to have my whole life change, the thing I was most afraid of being the truth had finally arrived.

Poison oak ravaged his body with infected rashes, and he got Giardia drinking from what the Big Sur locals call "a natural spring," but which was just a rusty pipe pouring water onto the highway at mile marker 42. I told him not to drink from it, but he didn't listen. The parasite dwindled him down to skin and bones. Then both our bodies were unrecognizable to each other.

The Startle

Suddenly, Ladybird halted and sat down, looking spooked and wanting me to lead. When I caught up to her I saw a deer on its side, eyes open, organs exploded from its chest, limbs bent in the wrong directions. I tiptoed towards it, a habit of being quiet around its living brethren, even though it was very far from living. I crouched down and stared into its brown eyes, permanently caught in their startle, the startle a split second before its life was smacked out of it, its innards torn outwards after tangling with metal and glass.

I leapt behind a tree and choked out all of my bile and booze from the night before, then dropped in the mess of wet pine needles to catch my breath. The dog cocked her head at me, frightened. I comforted her, steadied myself, rounded the tree and found a turkey vulture descended on the deer, feasting on its heart.

Staircase

Daniel and I met on a staircase. He was ascending it as I stood on the top step and we immediately started talking as though in mid-conversation, effortlessly, joyously. He was on tour, doing lights for a band I was going to see perform that night.

He lived in New York, where I was moving and only knew a few people, and once I arrived he was the first person I called. He introduced me to the bar where I became a regular, had a permanent barstool and never once paid for a drink, but where I always left a huge tip. He introduced me to his friends, who also became mine. He eventually introduced me to his girlfriend, who I didn't know existed. We proceeded as friends and I pretended not to feel a twinge when I walked into a party and saw him kissing her, and I hoped he felt the same twinge when he walked to my barstool and found me kissing a series of musicians whose sole topic of conversation was their own bands.

A couple of years later, Daniel announced he was moving to L.A. We spent his last few weeks in New York letting the pretense fall away now that we were both single, until his last night in town, a humid one in August, and walked the streets of the East Village holding each other's sweaty hands and kissing on every corner. When he arrived in California, he called me to say, "I'm sitting under the orange tree in my new backyard and you should be here."

Instead, we met back in Seattle, where we had met on that staircase, and ate Chinese food overlooking the water. My fortune cookie read *Your lover will be true to you*, and I kept the slip of paper in my wallet for the next ten years, even as it disintegrated. I always assumed it was about Daniel.

The Nurse

Early on, Daniel swept his thumb over my areola, observing the faint red bumps that surrounded my nipples. "What are these tiny red bumps? They respond to my touch." I didn't know, and had never noticed them. We researched it together, and found that they were glands for lubrication for breastfeeding. As if my maternity was predetermined, whether or not my body was actually the vessel I would use to nurture.

When you're with somebody whose mother can't be their mother, you become their mother. Daniel needed stability at home, delicious cooking smells, warmth, music, a dog to love—all of the things to come home to that he didn't have when he was growing up. But, like they do their real parents, they all start to resent you for it. They always need to have their foot out the door, an escape route, just like children do as they become teenagers and see their parents as flawed, aggravating, humiliating beings tethering them to one place, one family, one way of existing.

I thought the resentment of a real parent would be replaced by gratitude. But now, like an aged parent of adult children, I live a solitary life in my silent cabin where the phone rings perfunctorily instead of passionately.

There's selfishness in my selflessness, my

mothering. The only way to be indispensable, valued, validated, is to be needed by others, to provide a service. My body wants maternity, wants to labor, and my brain knows it's because of the ultimate hedonism: babies always have something to cry for, to need—their survival is contingent on being held.

Memories and visions of maternity appear when I'm ovulating each month, recurring dreams of laboring and birthing. I know I'm in the fertile window of my menstrual cycle when I close my eyes and a vision appears from a childhood home video: my parents are testing out a new video camera, and my mom is holding me, eight months old, in her arms. My mom and dad kiss and wave for the camera, and then my mom spins in slow circles with me, dancing with her baby, just the two of us in her world, though my dad and sister are a foot away. She bounces me on her hip as she twirls, and we both giggle with joy, our mother-daughter dance in our cocoon that belongs just to us.

For hours after I've held a baby, I find myself swaying back and forth as though I'm still holding them, soothing them, making them feel cherished.

Milagros y Sangre

I had hidden a tin Mexican wedding milagro, a lucky charm with a bride and groom on it, in the beams of our cabin when Daniel and I first moved in. I cradled it in my hands and whispered a blessing into it before tucking it away above the fireplace to watch over us. The milagro came from a voodoo shop in the middle of the forest in Northern California, next to the world's smallest church. We got tarot readings in the church, where only one of us could physically fit at a time.

"This is my mean tarot deck. A nasty one. But it's the most honest," the tarot reader told me. My anxious giggle blew out a candle.

"The death of something is coming. You will ride the death rattle for a long time."

Daniel carefully climbed into the church after I jumped out, unable to find my sea legs for a minute. The willow trees in the garden had cobalt blue bottles hanging from them, to catch evil spirits. I backed away from them and went into the shop, where I found the milagro and a voodoo cookbook.

"She told me the death of something is coming," I told Daniel when we got back in the car. His face was bright white. He looked ill. I could see him swallow as he nodded with a strange, disconnected enthusiasm.

"What did she tell you?" I asked, my voice too

loud, my body suddenly energetic and hot.

"Oh, I don't know. Nothing much."

The voodoo cookbook had a spell to return your lover to you. I found it as I desperately turned every page of every book in the cabin's shelves. Daniel had a habit of leaving items as bookmarks between the pages after he'd finished reading a book—post-cards, boarding passes, something to mark where he had been or what time period he'd been reading it. I clawed through the pages of the voodoo cookbook, desperate to find something he'd left behind that would give me any insight into what had happened. I laughed at the love spell, before realizing I was desperate enough to try it.

I collected my menstrual blood and put it in the freezer, awaiting a waxing moon. Menstrual blood, the book explained, held the deepest of pheromones, and could bind my love to me. The blood froze into a heart shape in the corner of the plastic bag. On the night of the waxing moon, I lit seven candles, boiled three liters of water, and taped a photo of Daniel to the bathroom mirror, as instructed. When the water boiled, I added seven teaspoons of salt, and stirred it for seven minutes with the turmeric-stained wooden spoon. I poured the water into the stopped sink, added my seven drops of melted menstrual blood, and submerged my hands, chanting the spell as I bore my eyes into his image until I was hoarse. I unplugged the drain, took down the picture, washed the pot and spoon, blew out the candles, and winked at the moon. I believed he would come back to me.

Ashes and Altars

The spell didn't bring Daniel back. Instead, my period disappeared for seven months, unkindly punctuating that I couldn't take care of myself, let alone anyone else. When it returned, my body felt waterlogged, unbearably heavy, grotesque. The wedding milagro in the beams reminded me of its existence in a dream, and at 5am I teetered on a chair as I reached up to remove it. A gray spider living on it spun in violent circles, threatened by the vibrations my fingers sent down its web. The milagro still had its price tag, which made it feel suddenly impure. I tossed it in the fireplace, the clang of tin against the metal grates echoing, the loudest sound in our cabin in months. I cackled as my whiskey-sallowed face got too close to the milagro melting.

An unholy splatter in the middle of the street. My first reaction was embarrassment, like I'd walked in on something private. Someone else's blood, their absolute interior, wasn't mine to see. Their unintentional killer had taken great care when moving them to the side of the road. Two tiny baby raccoons, laying side by side. At their feet, an altar of four branches. Their rigor mortis made them look like they were dancing, singing along to a song. One of them had its tongue hanging out, almost in joy. A classic teen girl pose—dance till we drop.

Memories of Body

I know Big Sur in my bones, in my skin, in the scar on my throat from when I was a baby. The jagged, rocky coastline that I've adored and feared since conscious memory. I was baptized by fire there at six weeks old. My parents took me camping, swaddled and tiny and new. They and their friends made a bonfire, my mom holding me in her arms. The fire popped, and they thought that's what made me cry, but as my howls became more guttural and feral, they realized an ember had jumped from the fire to my throat. My mom and I were both inconsolable, I've been told for years. The scar is six weeks younger than me, but it's been with me almost my whole life, right in the crease where my throat turns into my neck. It changes shape and depth as my body changes, and sometimes I try to swat it away when I see it in the mirror before realizing it's just my scar, looking unrecognizable on my inconsistent body.

We camped there every summer when I was a child, packing up our yellow Volvo station wagon with tents and coolers in our driveway in Salinas. My sister and I dutifully held our breath every time we crossed the Bixby Bridge, each time racing each other to tell the story first of the man on the prison crew who built it, who fell into one of the pillars while the cement was being poured. We claimed to be able to see the outline of his hand, grasping from the inside, and he would haunt the campsite at night if we didn't hold our breath over his early grave. I never bothered to research this story later in life, never felt the need to verify it. It was as real as my purple and green plaid sleeping bag, as the poison oak I carefully avoided.

We ate cereal from flimsy paper bowls, washed our hands at the spigot on the edge of the campsite, and hiked up to the gorge with the dead pine needles crunching beneath our water shoes that released a cool, wooded scent I can access anywhere in the world when I think of it. The hike to the gorge seemed endless as a child, but the payoff of the cool water in the swimming hole at the top of the hike was worth the trek, worth the river crossing, worth our screeching when mating dragonflies buzzed around our heads.

In the afternoons, we peeled off our wet bathing suits in our tent and changed into clothes for soccer, kickball and tag, rode our bikes to the general store to buy candy, and made friends with the other camping kids our ages. At night, after a propane stove dinner, we went to the ranger's campfire, where ghost stories were told under the centuries-old redwood trees.

Everything tasted and smelled better in Big Sur: the Ambrosiaburger at Nepenthe lived up to its name; the taste of instant hot chocolate temporarily alleviated the itch of our bug bites; root beers we were allowed to drink in the afternoons, swaying in a hammock, have never been so crisp or refreshing since then. Pfeiffer Beach smelled salty, from the white water crashing on the signature black sand, but also sweet, from the sun-heated rocks and kelp. The first time I smelled marijuana was in Big Sur, sitting in the river in a giant wood chair, reading a chapter book about a witch child who made her own elixirs to heal people. I thought I was smelling one of her healing ointments as I read about them, so mysterious and herbal.

There lived the Henry Miller Memorial Library, which seemed too dreamy to be real, with its monstrous redwood trees, fairy lights, persimmon tree, green grass, ping pong table, resident cats, and a cabin full of books for all the artistic interlopers to choose from and talk about. This was where I first brought Daniel when he came to California to meet my family; I had to bring him to Big Sur. I had to show him this place exists, this place is me, this is who I am, and what I smell, and what I see, and what I feel, this is what I carry with me. This place that soothes and scares me, this place that has the most welcoming people and the most treacherous land, this place that falls apart every few years to reject too many visitors, to preserve its history and its pristineness. I couldn't believe it was real, or that I was real, until the person I loved saw it and knew it, too.

I drove Daniel to the black sand beach, where we giggled as the wind whipped our hair across our faces, and we ducked for cover behind a rock and kissed as the wind howled. I took him to Nepenthe, where we sat by the fire, looked at photo albums of the locals drinking martinis at the bar in the 1950s, and Daniel shared a pot of tea with my mom. I could see Big Sur worked the same way on him that it did on me.

Ten years later, Daniel and I snuck into a pot farm across the street from the Henry Miller Library to take our wedding photos, because that piece of land had the best view. The man living in his VW bus working as a lookout saw us and opened the gate, giving us his congratulations, and added a marijuana leaf to my bouquet. During our wedding dinner, Daniel got up from our table and didn't return. He'd sat down at another table to talk to some friends. That night, back in our hotel room we couldn't afford, he told me he was going to go to sleep, so I finished eating a piece of cake, sitting by myself in my wedding dress. Even then I didn't know, didn't realize. I was so accustomed to accepting him, his reasons, his excuses. The next morning he wasn't next to me when I woke up and I found him by the river, jittery, ready to hit the road, anxious to keep moving. We drove the six hours back to Los Angeles in silence. I didn't want to speak first.

Commune

Daniel's new job was at a commune that held retreats, everything from photography lessons to meditation retreats to grief workshops. Its roots included first wave hippies and Eastern meditation, along with a legendary stint of Hunter S. Thompson as the security guard at the front gate. The staff mostly lived onsite in cabins, and most of them never left once they got there. It was perched on a cliff above the ocean, an hour and a half drive to the closest grocery store or doctor. Meals were served in a big, communal dining room, where any time you walked in you might see one person crying, another person close to climaxing, and definitely someone playing guitar or a more esoteric instrument. The food was heavenly; the nectar of the gods, all made from the onsite farm and garden.

This place was part of my body of celestial memories from Big Sur as a child, when my family went for open weekends held for locals. We hiked up the river, made flower crowns sitting on the lawn, ate plates of food heaped with rice and curry made from the freshly picked garden vegetables, homemade wheat sourdough bread with fresh fruit jams from the orchard, drank the richest coconut milk hot cocoa when the fog came in. This was the first place I saw a man naked in real life, by the pool, as my sister and I giggled and stole glances at his penis while he dove into the water and did a handstand. The commune was clothing optional, and it was famous most of all for its adults-only natural hot springs. As a teenager, I regularly partook in the midnight bathing offered to locals, from 1-3am every weeknight. This was the first place I saw lots of people naked in real life, and people in various states of seduction and power, and men pretending to be harmless.

After that first early visit to Big Sur, Daniel and I returned regularly over the years, and I eventually took Daniel to the midnight baths at the commune, at the southernmost point of Big Sur. There was a meteor shower, and we sat supine in the tubs, watching for the meteors, listening to the waves crashing on the rocks fifty feet below us. We got home at 5am, ate peanut butter chocolate cookies I'd made earlier, slept until noon. When we woke up he picked a fight with me and returned to the cabin he was renting in Big Sur for six weeks to figure out what he wanted to do with his life. I'd found him the cabin through a friend's family. That night, a French tourist drove off the Bixby Bridge on his motorcycle and the Coast Guard spent a week trying to find his body, to no avail. When Daniel resurfaced and asked me to come visit him in the cabin, I drove over the bridge just as a crane was pulling up the mangled motorcycle from the rocks.

While Daniel made us whole wheat pancakes on his propane stove perched on the edge of the deck, I flipped through the roll of photos he'd had developed from the last week. Photos of the fog, of his feet, a close up of a fern, Lucky—the dog he was minding—and, forgotten in the roll, a photo of a naked woman in the middle of having sex with Daniel, shot from his perspective.

Adrenaline carried me through our pancake dinner. Like the other times I'd found a new woman's face in a roll of his photographs, or heard a new woman's name leave his lips, my instinct was to be measured, methodical. I would prove myself wrong about what I'd seen or heard, and I wouldn't have to choose between living with knowing a new truth, or confronting Daniel. After we'd washed the dishes in the makeshift sink on the deck, Daniel told me he was tired and going to sleep early. As soon as the light from his propane lantern faded, I found the negatives to the roll of photos and saw the story: a photo of this woman at the beach in a typical tourist shot, then naked on a bed, then euphoric while being fucked by Daniel, then posing wet and dripping in the shower. Because I was looking at the negatives, everything was opposite and she looked like a monster with no teeth and an angry face. But I'd seen the one forgotten developed photo in the roll and knew that wasn't true. I could tell which beach they'd been on when he'd taken the tourist photo of her, and so I knew that it was near the commune, and I already knew the parts of the story that weren't shown in the photos: her perky breasts, bobbing in and out of the water of the hot springs, him acting harmless while he hunted her.

Daniel, the photographer who rarely took photos of me, had documented one of his affairs and was either too lazy or too cruel to hide it from me. I had spent years fine tuning the neglect of my own instincts surrounding Daniel's infidelities. It always happened at a time when I was too tired to have my whole life change around me, so instead, I went to sleep next to him.

As a child, I was completely unaware of the undercurrent at the commune. The hot springs, the food, the disconnection from the world made it a place free of law, morals or obligations. Many of the staff literally never left—people who "worked" and lived there for thirty years who hadn't been off property in twenty-eight years, who lived in perpetuity in the Summer of Love. People who, Daniel would later marvel, "had totally different lives before they came here, but those lives don't even matter." The staff and its visitors all thrive on this perceived "freedom." Everyone dates or just fucks each other, mostly in places they'll be seen doing so.

Early in his employment, I spent the day at the commune, and as Daniel's shift finished, he suggested we jump in the pool before driving home. I deferred at first, uncomfortable being naked together in front of six of his coworkers. That I would be uncomfortable with this was mocked, and I eventually gave in. I mutely removed my clothes and stepped into the pool as his coworkers inspected and commented on every inch of my cold, naked body. I wanted the pool water to force itself into my lungs, to drown instead of having to get out in front of their predatory eyes. Daniel swam away from me.

Later, he chastised me for not being involved enough with his life at the commune. I pushed back that he was too involved, and that it was OK for me not to feel comfortable or normal being naked in front of his coworkers.

"Name one other job in the world where it's normal for your wife and coworkers to be naked together," I insisted.

"There isn't one," he replied.

"Exactly."

"That's what makes it so special," he proclaimed. His superiority was palpable. He was unabashedly in love with the place, spent more and more hours there, infiltrating each department. He befriended the janitorial staff and was invited to their secret steak and whiskey night. He began a flirtation, and eventual sexual relationship, with a woman in the I.T. department who had taken on a Native American name, but whose real name was Rebecca. He finally won over the oldest, grumpiest member of the staff, the man who ran the art yurt. Daniel began to stay later and later at the commune each night, working on art pieces with him.

"They started calling me the Oracle," Daniel told me after returning home from work one night. I stifled a laugh when I realized he was proud of this and not horrified and amused by it, like I was.

At the center of the commune's functions and philosophies was a weekly group therapy session for each staff department called "Process." Every Wednesday, when Daniel's department had their Process, I came to expect an increasing stretch of silence from him. During the first few sessions, he came home at the end of his workday and reported some of it back to me—Sandra and Soren had been having tension in the office, and when the Process practitioner confronted them about it, he told Sandra she was holding her resentment in her chest, and Soren that he was holding his in his jaw. He pressed on their bodies in these spots, and each crumbled into tears, Daniel said.

In the beginning, he seemed as skeptical of it as to wonder if this was a performance, some kind of initiation they were doing—a prank on Daniel, the new hire. After a few sessions, he reported to me that Christine was having trouble in her marriage, a marriage to another woman who lived and worked at the commune, and they were going to move into different yurts and intentionally fuck other people and take a vow of silence from each other for six weeks. Process was, apparently, all about the here and now. Forget your past, don't think about the future—the only way to best serve yourself and your life was to be completely present. Surrender entirely to what you want and who you are at any given moment. Talking or thinking about one's past and how it affected their present was futile, pedestrian, a waste of time, and surrendering to what you want in the present moment every moment was the only way to be aware, the only way to exist.

Once Daniel was sold on Process, he absorbed it wholly. His coworkers were not just seeing his naked body and sharing that act of exterior intimacy every day, but they were now getting his interior intimacy, too. He stopped telling me anything about Process, except to gloat about how incredible the sessions were, what a special group of humans he spent his days with. He had post-Process meetings—dates, really—with some of his coworkers. He'd allude to a special conversation he'd had with Christine sitting on a grassy hill, drinking tea and weaving feathers into each other's hair. He began to crow about "The Human Potential Movement," another belief system held in the highest esteem at the commune.

Frantic and embarrassed that I didn't know any of these new words or ideas in his daily life, I dutifully wrote down and researched all the phrases he brought into our home and listened for hours to him ruminating about how evolved these people were, how being "present" and only giving a fuck about yourself in any moment was the way to reach maximum potential. Inevitably I would ask the wrong question, and he'd look at me like I was a human who would never reach any kind of potential.

I stopped doing the research and asking any questions, though I became increasingly aware of the fact that he was spending all of his "present" time with other people: people who had left behind cities, jobs, responsibilities, and several who had left their own children to live in an exclusive Utopia. A place where you could grow your own food and drugs—opium being the preferred homegrown drug—where you could never see another newspaper for the rest of your life, a place where phones didn't work, where everyone was naked and free of any morals, judgments, or burdens.

In researching the methods and tenets of the Process, I found hope in the last one—that its practitioners had to take responsibility for their actions and feelings. I waited for Daniel to get to that step, to recalibrate and see that being present and having a conscience could coexist. He didn't reach it before he left me. He told me he sat in a chair in the house of Fritz Perls, the man who originated this school of thought or therapy. Daniel sat there for three days, feeling Fritz's presence, feeling the emotional weight of it. This meant nothing to me, and still doesn't. He wanted this to mean something to me, and I wanted it to mean less to him. He wanted me to be astounded by this intensity, and I wanted him to ask me about my day. I wanted to rip that feather out of his hair and eat it, so it could travel my body and belong to me, so I could shit it out.

Daniel couldn't have, wouldn't have become The Oracle without me. My life was dedicated to his divination, and I was relentless in my desire to be the architect of his happiness. Before the commune, I got him a job running an enormous, ornate, insanely beautiful Spanish Gothic theater built in 1926, founded by Mary Pickford, Douglas Fairbanks, and Charlie Chaplin in downtown Los Angeles. He became obsessed with it, in a way that made me feel an absurd jealousy of an old building. The attention he paid to its details was envy-making: the restoration of a small piece of a statue in the lobby, his climbing through the duct work, ascending to the very heights of the auditorium, up above the heavy glass chandelier. He knew every centimeter of this humongous theater better than the centimeters of my body.

He fixated on it in a way that gave him purpose, but when something went wrong there, he was shattered. An event went badly because the organizer hadn't listened to Daniel's recommendations, and he was so morose telling me about it on the phone when I called to tell him I was coming home from a party, I was convinced he was going to commit suicide. I barreled through every red light in Los Angeles and was consumed with fear as I raced into our house, leaving the front door open, preparing to find his dead body. I had been wrong, but not so wrong: he was in bed, where he remained for forty-eight hours.

He remained so catatonic that I researched and found "The Best Psychiatrist in Los Angeles," and broke down his door on Labor Day to get him to talk to Daniel and write him a prescription that might do something. The psychiatrist eventually told me he had never seen a lion in Los Angeles and it had frightened him, and at first I didn't realize he meant me.

Shortly after our wedding, Daniel decided it was time to leave the city and our jobs, and finally move to Big Sur. We would have a new life, wide open spaces, and start our family. There was only one place he wanted to work: the commune. I began my hunt, pursuing old family friends and peripheral acquaintances. He sent resume after resume, all of which I edited. He got the call after I tracked down a particular former acquaintance who had once worked there. Daniel and I rehearsed the job interview ad nauseam—I asked interview questions until he became frustrated, and then asked more. He got the second interview. He drove the six hours to Big Sur after working a shift at his job until midnight, did the interview, and drove the six hours back. He got a speeding ticket for driving over 100 miles an hour. But he'd done it, and now we waited for the final word, the ruling on his future happiness. He had been convinced for years Big Sur was the only place he'd be happy, and if he just put the time in, he'd eventually earn it, or deserve it, or be ready for it. And so we waited. I left my long line of jobs of being a minder and mother to the rich and famous, and began taking any kind of freelance writing job I could wrangle—ghostwriting cookbooks, editing resumes, writing copy for a cosmetics company—so we could easily move if he got the offer.

A couple of weeks after the speeding ticket, the front door opened as I sat in our living room reading, but nobody entered the house. I jumped up from my chair in fear. A single cardboard box came through the front door and I knew what it meant: he'd gotten the job. We were moving. He'd planned on telling me this way, with the single moving box, for weeks. We screamed and kissed and made gin and tonics and packed that first box.

Our last night in LA, our friend Nora hosted a goodbye party for us in her backyard, where toddlers and dogs and chickens ran around underneath the string lights, the orange trees with their blossoms releasing their scent into the hot night. I had never been sad to leave a town before, usually moving when I was past ready to move on. That night I felt panic rise repeatedly in my throat, so concrete it was hard to swallow the beer I was pounding. I couldn't figure out why: we had a place to live, we both had jobs, we knew this place we were moving to, we had longed for it for years. But I felt terror. I watched all of our friends in that backyard and felt explosive sadness for everything I would miss, and miss out on. I watched Daniel peacock about the job he was leaving and the job he was about to start, inflating his story as always. I used to think this was a trait of his enthusiasm for something, but over the years, the exaggerations just turned into lies.

We packed our cars and drove separately, leaving over an hour apart from each other. This disjointed departure and arrival were indicative of what had begun to happen that I couldn't see. The division, the separation, began far sooner for him than I ever realized. I was too busy always clearing the path ahead of him and cleaning up behind him to make sure he would find happiness along the way.

And so the Oracle arrived at the commune. My first orchestration was telling him about the best bakery in town, and to go get a pink, butter-stained bakery box to bring with him his first day of work. It was a success. Within weeks he would retell the story of the tiny pastel French tarts and macarons as his own idea, eliminating me from it.

A series of hand-carved wood signs posted every twenty feet on the fence at the commune separate the hills from the ocean cliffs. The signs read "Extreme danger." I remember laughing at them— the signmaker had put effort into making the cursive script beautiful and non-threatening, though the words were harsh. I took a picture of one of them, the sea behind it and stalks of pampas grass in front of it, gently waving in the wind.

Bridge

Big Sur began its traditional cycle of expelling roads and mountains from itself, with entire portions of Highway 1 being wiped out by landslides. Just a few months before, the Soberanes Fire had burned 100,000 acres of land, and now there were streams of black ash pouring down the hills that used to boast centuries-old trees. The rains, which we all begged for during that endless fire, were near Biblical, destroying the limited infrastructure of the tiny, wild community. On the weekend before Valentine's Day, a man living under the Pfeiffer Bridge saw that it was buckling in half, the pylons caving in towards each other. His alert to authorities caused the bridge to be shut to anyone but locals, as they brought out crews of engineers to forge the wilds and inspect it. It would need to come down. There would be no way to drive in or out of Big Sur for close to a year. No tourists could come in. Children living in Big Sur couldn't get to their schools in Carmel or Monterey. Everyone would have to make a choice about which side they would stay on: north or south. If you chose south, you had to be willing to live without medications, food, and propane deliveries. Come February 15th the bridge would be closed to everyone, demolished, and rebuilt. Residents could drive their cars, one car on the bridge at a time, north or south, once they chose a side.

Daniel walked out of Big Sur, over the bridge and left his car on the south side. I picked him up—it was pitch black out, nighttime in the forest. He was holding a flashlight, and I knew it was him by the way the light was swinging to the rhythm of his walk.

He came home, packed some bags, and slept on the couch. In the morning on February 14th, Daniel wept as he said goodbye to Ladybird.

"I forgot, I found this for you in the free box at the commune," he said as he wiped his tears and handed me a blue wool sweater.

He grabbed his bag and I drove him to the bridge crossing. He ran into someone he knew and they started to walk over the bridge together. He gave me a distracted hug goodbye. The Oracle decided to be the savior of the commune, of the land. He sequestered himself on his side of the bridge, while I remained on mine. When he did speak to me, it was to tell me tales of organizing helicopter rescue missions for sixty-five people who were stranded there, or saving a stroke victim, or deciding who at the commune would be removed and who would be allowed to stay. Delusions of grandeur, lies, or truth, I will never know. There are so many blurred lines with an Oracle. He only needed me to be his audience now, and when I deigned to push back against him, he chose a vow of silence, to me exclusively. We were not going to speak to each other for six weeks, while he continued to be worshiped and continued to wor-ship my replacement and continued to worship himself and continued to lie to anyone who crossed his path who didn't believe he was worthy of idolatry.

For six weeks we didn't speak. I wept. My body disappeared. Some days it felt like it was disintegrating from the inside out, when I stopped getting my period and when the nurses and doctors looked alarmed and retested my blood pressure. Other days it felt like it was disintegrating from the outside in, as when my hair began to grow in completely gray overnight, like Leland Palmer, and then just started falling out.

I began stumbling on the dead almost daily. First, a mangled snake on the beach, tangled into itself over and over again. And then the raccoons, birds, deer, mice, frogs, a fanged fish, lizards, a butterfly, squirrels. All left to rot, just like me. My rotting body, just carrion clinging to my bones. I felt like I had to acknowledge these beings that were now carcasses, acknowledge them in death to honor their life. At night, I heard the neighborhood cats screaming, like they were being torn to shreds. Every morning I walked the hills to find them, and every morning, each of them was still alive, though every night they'd scream, "This is the end!" and it echoed through the canyon.

First I tried to sleep through the weeks, taking every pill the doctor would give me to finally fall asleep each night. Then I tried to live through it, running as fast as I could through the sand on the beach with Ladybird until I couldn't breathe, until

my body made me stop, my torn ankle tendons floating around like flotsam and jetsam. I couldn't eat, my
throat closing itself to anything but the bottles of li-
quor I poured down it every night, first once the sun
set, then while it was setting, then at any time of day
to try to make it bearable to be alive. Every night, hot
and humming from the alcohol, I would hope not to
wake up in the morning—the path of least resistance.

When I had to drive anywhere, I did so too
fast, carelessly, too close to the edge, just hoping.
I'd go as far as I could south to Big Sur, before the
missing bridge, to see if it was time yet for my bap-
tism by fire to be completed, for my body's rejection
from this place to be brought to its inevitable end. I
begged for the Bixby Bridge to crack under my tires
and swallow me, for a landslide to expel me from the
mountains into the sea. I stared up at the redwoods
that were heavy with rain, and imagined one of them
turning into a guillotine in a swift fall. I waited for
a wildfire to finish the job it had started on my neck
and turn me to charcoal.

Some days I wanted to live and I wanted him
to turn to ash instead of me. All days, I woke up and
gasped when I remembered what my life had suddenly become. I wondered if it ever really existed the
way I remembered it. There was nobody else who
would testify to it, because Daniel had turned into
the Oracle, and The Oracle wasn't there.

Predictable

I never had to imagine it because I saw it. She shook my hand, saw me in my three dimensions and I watched as a bystander while the three of us transformed from a "we" to a "me" to a "them." Only occasionally did I let myself wonder if he ever accidentally called her by my nickname, maybe a reflex after using the same term of endearment for so many years. Maybe he does it often enough that it's now her nickname. Maybe he's never uttered the word again.

I needed to go somewhere I'd never been with him. When I imagined it, I saw myself on a boat, freezing, and knew it had to be Chicago. A place I'd always wanted to go, a place whose architecture could loom like giants over me, protecting me. Where no memory would surface and smother me. I booked a flight leaving the next day.

"I'm going somewhere," I told him. "I can't be here. I'm going somewhere and I don't want to tell you where," losing composure telling him the last part. I'd never withheld something from him, had always wanted to share everything with him.

"You're going to Chicago," he said wearily.

"How did you know?" I asked, stunned.

"Because I know you." He seemed annoyed, disappointed that I hadn't chosen something unpredictable instead.

The morning of my flight, we took Ladybird on a walk together at the beach. I tried to keep pace with them, but my recently torn ankle tendons could barely manage the sand. When he stopped to look at a shell, I caught up with him and tried to talk, but he just shrugged in response. I laughed alone at Ladybird throttling a littered plastic water bottle. This was suddenly no longer our family, our routine.

Daniel was at work a couple of months earlier when I had missed the last step going down a flight of stairs and landed on my side on the floor, my ankle pulsing with pain. When I told him about it that night, saying, "I think there's something really wrong with it," he began his nightly monologue about his work day. Weeks later, when I began going to physical therapy twice a week, he was surprised. "Physical therapy? For what?" I had a nightmare about him sinking his teeth into my leg and tearing out the tendons as they flopped and bounced, hanging from his jaws.

My flight and hotel in Chicago barely made a dent in our shared savings account, because nobody vacations in Chicago in January. I could see into the hotel across the street from mine. There was a businessman having breakfast, his suitcase behind him. His white shirt appeared crisp from afar, but was probably rumpled with travel and exhaustion up close. Something about his dichotomous fatigue and freshness felt attainable. If he could wake up and put on his wrinkled shirt, give his presentation, then make his flight with time to be home for dinner, maybe I could make it, too. Maybe there was a similar tenacity buried somewhere in my wrinkled clothes, in my desperate exhaustion.

My grief pulsated through me, keeping my blood hot, and I couldn't get enough cold air to combat it. I spent three hours in the Art Institute, as an exercise in finding out what I like without Daniel's influence. I played a game with myself to see how far into the Institute I could get without fainting in public, trying to thwart my panic, my lack of blood sugar. I came upon a dark room with a gold dragon glowing behind glass and sat down until another museum-goer entered. I couldn't bear to be there with someone else, or in any room with a person who wasn't Daniel.

Next, the Field Museum was too big, spread out, depleting. I tried to live in my newfound appreciation for certain types of birds in the Bird Hall, but their calls were piped through the speakers and I could feel their feathers smothering me. I backed away, greeted by lions and armadillos, then on to the snakes. I wanted to coil around Daniel and strangle the betrayals from his body.

Daniel always told me I was scared of everything, jumpy, and ruled by fear. When he left, fear seemed extraneous, silly. I didn't mind the spiders in the shower, I climbed the roof when it was still wet from rain, I let Ladybird go so far away from me at the beach, I cohabitated with unknown rodents in the basement who kept me up all night, I drove too fast, I drank too much, I took pills; I resided in my former fears. He didn't know this version of me at all.

But I knew him. I knew he always had an escape plan, most often to the woods or desert, somewhere nobody could reach him. I knew he'd developed a nervous swallow at the end of his sentences since he joined the commune. I knew he didn't like giving anything a second chance: people, restaurants. I knew that being in the middle of nowhere was a challenge that felt good to him. I knew he just wanted to be left alone most of the time. I knew he just wanted it to be easy. I knew being alone, or with a new person who didn't know any of this seemed like the easiest thing to do.

I knew his name started falling off the envelopes that used to be addressed to both of us.

Hallmark

It was nice knowing you. The message was scrawled inside a sympathy card that Daniel's mother sent me. It, blissfully, mercifully, was likely the last communication I'd ever receive from her. I could imagine her writing it in her dark apartment, because she never changed the lightbulbs when they burned out. It allowed her not to see the stains from spills she would never clean, the ribbon shavings from an art project, the moldy oranges she put out as a centerpiece and forgot about. Underneath her signature, she wrote *(Daniel's Mom)*. After twelve years, she believed this was a necessary clarification.

Occasions

There were the dates, and the milestones associated with them, that marked the devolution of Daniel and me. Cruelly, humorously, they're mostly holidays, dates acknowledged every year by the general population.

On Halloween, Daniel spent the day getting costumes for us. We were going to the legendary Halloween party at Nepenthe restaurant that had been around since the Jack Kerouac and Henry Miller days, to drink and dance and eat free Ambrosiaburgers on the foggy decks above the sea. As the day drew to a close, and the party became imminent, Daniel's mood fouled.

"Do you not want to go? Do you not want to see your new coworkers at a party like this?" I was trying to understand the reason, if there was one.

"No, it's OK. We'll go."

He dressed me as a demon: he draped my head and body with a large, black cloak; painted my face white, with ghoulish black eyes; and secured a long, gray beard to my mouth with an elastic strap. He dressed me as a demon, and then didn't look at me or speak to me the rest of the night. He dressed me as a demon, and his young, morally ambiguous coworkers flitted around him, naked but for the glitter pasties of their mermaid costumes. He dressed me as a demon, and danced with the mermaids.

Then it was Thanksgiving, on which Daniel volunteered to work overnight at the security gate on the commune's property. He called it a rite of passage, and I hadn't seen him so thrilled in months. He visibly ached his way through the family Thanksgiving dinner, could not make it more evident how desperately he wanted to leave. Later, I learned that was the week he met her, but I would never learn whether the overnight shift was a reality or a ruse.

Over Christmas, we moved into our dream home, spending that week prepping the cabin, having a fence built to make a yard for Ladybird, washing the windows, and patching up the paint. One day, an enormous planter, several hundred pounds, rolled directly onto the walking path and smashed. Pieces of shattered teal ceramic littered the pathway and blocked the front door. When a repair man came to look at the chimney, I gazed out the window just as he fell off the roof—his body flying down, a sickening thud. I forced him to stay still and cradled his head until the air returned to his lungs, until he could see if he could still move his extremities. I didn't admit to myself that these seemed like bad signs. I was sick of signs, exhausted from intimating higher meanings from everything.

We forged ahead. I spent our moving day watching Daniel rolling his eyes and barking and chest-puffing to the movers in a way I'd seen his mother do. His movements seemed almost boxer-like; circling his opponent around the ring, waiting to strike, taunting. Why were the movers his opponents? I didn't understand. Simultaneously, he unpacked an enormous painting and found a spot for it nestled in between a wall of windows and the built-in bookshelves.

"Honey. It fits perfectly. Perfectly! It was made for this house," he beamed, kissed me, massaged my sore moving shoulders. After tipping the movers astronomically to make up for Daniel's cantankerous behavior, I saw him standing in the corner of the bedroom, looking out the skylight. The view of him in our bedroom evoked an immediate feeling, and I saw the word "TEMPORARY" floating through my head. I was so startled by this forcible vision, I gasped. Daniel looked at me inquisitively.

That night, Christmas Eve, was the first time we had sex in our new home, and it was the last time we would ever have sex, the last time Daniel would move towards me. It was oddly quiet. I didn't know what had just happened, but it didn't feel like him. He was a stranger. He was temporary.

New Year's Eve. The night I shook hands with her, when some of it started to become clear to me. The night I saw them, learned that there was a them. The next morning, shell-shocked, still trying to claim my space and my life with Daniel, I stayed for a few hours at the commune. I went to the hot spring tub on the roof, the one that not everybody knew about, and climbed in before realizing the water was cold. While running new, hot water into it, I brought my knees up to my chest, and reluctantly looked out at the ocean. In that moment I didn't want to see its beauty. From a baby owl the night before, to a mother whale and baby whale playing together in the waves that morning. Their tails synchronized as they flipped their beautiful, large bodies down to dive back into the water. A mama and her baby, but no father.

Wanting to become a mother had been written into my biology in recent years, evolving from a distant possibility to a sharp, clear desire, ultimately transforming into the physical symptom of my eyes leaking tears whenever I interacted with a child. It didn't feel like a decision or a choice I made. I felt the wanting in my body—it had bypassed my brain. And maybe it wasn't even wanting to become a mother to a child, but suddenly I saw everything that everyone needed, and I felt a physical duty to be the one to provide it. That morning, the sight of the mother whale and her baby evoked a sob that came out of my throat sounding more like a guffaw.

And on Valentine's Day, Daniel walked south over the bridge.

Mercy

The car in front of mine swerved, so I mimicked it in anticipation of an unseen hazard. It avoided an unidentifiable brown, furry animal that had been hit, but not killed. I gasped as I saw it doing somersaults, writhing in pain. I couldn't give it the mercy of my tires.

Counsel

Enough locals grew restless in Big Sur that they forged an illegal hiking path to escape the island created by the fallen bridge. Daniel hiked out once a month to begrudgingly come to marriage counseling sessions with me. First we saw a young therapist in training because her facility charged a sliding scale, and Daniel wanted to pay the lowest dollar amount possible. The counselor took her shoes off during each appointment and rubbed her bare feet against the coffee table.

Occasionally, Daniel would hike out to stock up on medication, take a book from our shelves, or eat sushi by himself at our favorite restaurant. I ran into him at the drugstore, in the toothpaste aisle and we politely and awkwardly chatted, like acquaintances. When we parted ways, he forgot himself and gave me a wink, the way he did for years when we said goodbye to each other. The wink made me insist we try another counselor, and Daniel recommended someone he knew from the commune who had no official training or license, but who called himself "Dr. Love." He held sessions at his home, and there was no time limit. The first time and last time I subjected myself to this ridiculously monikered man, it was 100 degrees at his home office in Carmel Valley. I wore a new black silk dress, which absorbed so much of my sweat that it was permanently stained with white salt streaks by the end of the appointment.

Daniel and I sat together there for four hours. Dr. Love interjected in my tragic monologue here and there. At one point, he dramatically, with clear practice under his belt, proclaimed, "The first memory I have is my mother trying to abort me. That's a trauma I've had to live with since I was a fetus."

"Why are you so uptight about your husband having sex with other women?" Dr. Love asked me.

That's when I finally admitted there was nothing that would change the course Daniel set. We were permanently dismantled. When I got in my car at the end of the session, the mix of extreme heat and expelled tears made my face completely unrecognizable in my rearview mirror.

Rufus

I can pinpoint the moment the dismantling of our family began. Daniel and I drank gin in the ninety-degree Los Angeles heat, hours after the sun had set. We'd just put our dead dog's body in the car trunk of the veterinarian who came over to put him to sleep. She had wrapped Rufus in a blanket, leaving a hole for his sweet face. We put Daniel's sweatshirt in with Rufus to be cremated, the sweatshirt that had become the dog's as soon as we brought him home from the pound six years ago. Rufus came into our lives like this: I saw his photograph when we were beginning to think about adopting a dog, and I immediately burst into tears. The shelter said he had kennel cough and had to finish his course of treatment before he could be considered adoptable, so I called them every day for four weeks until he was better. We had never been to the shelter before, far east in the San Gabriel Valley, but as we exited the freeway to finally meet him I knew how to get there without needing the directions.

"How did you know how to get us here?" Daniel asked, somewhat bewildered.

"I just knew how to get to him," I responded, but I couldn't explain how.

The shelter said he was two years old, but he was more like seven years old, and our time with him turned out to be so much shorter than we anticipated. "He's got little old man veins," the vet said softly, as she tried to find an injection spot. Rufus was lying in his bed and we fed him tiny bits of steak, sobbing into his fur, thanking him over and over and over and over.

The night before, when we decided it was time, Daniel carried Rufus up the hill across the street from our house and the three of us watched the sunset together. Then we gave Rufus a warm bath, pausing to lean on our forearms and sob into the tub before resuming the gentle, loving cleansing of each part of his body for the last time. His barrel chest, his arthritic elbows and hips, his downturned tail, his perfect paws that smelled like popcorn. We poured some Sapporo into his water bowl, made him a little burger for dinner, and slept in our bed with him in between us. In the morning, he stayed in our bed, snoring loudly under the covers while we made him an omelet for breakfast.

The last photo I took of him was of my hand holding his paw on his last afternoon. In the photo, the professor patch on his elbow is visible. He had them on both elbows from sleeping on concrete at his previous owner's house. Rufus had a former life we knew nothing about, except that he ran away from it, and sometimes he would forget his new life and cower when we tried to pet his soft, velvety ears that were shaped like tortilla chips.

In the previous months, his dementia had made him swap day for night. We slept with the lights

on in the house so he could wander around safely, his
sight starting to go as well. I swapped day for night,
too, and rose multiple times a night to usher him out
from under tables and out of corners where he'd gotten stuck and confused. For months after he died, I
woke up to check the corners, forgetting, needing
still to take care of him.

Hobbies

In the nights I spent alone in our bed, I remember the things that made me feel sure. Daniel excelled at other people's birthdays. He hated his own; we both dreaded his birthday every year. I tried to make up for a childhood of broken birthdays, or I tried to honor his request to do something small, or nothing at all. His dad had remarried the day before Daniel's sixth birthday, and whatever I tried to make up for that was never successful.

He threw me two surprise parties that he secretly planned for months, never accepting help from anyone else. On my twenty-sixth birthday, he pulled into the parking lot at the Moonlight Rollerway in Glendale, and with a grin whispered, "Surprise." When we walked inside, roller skates in hand, all of my friends were cheering for me and rollerskating, two giant gold balloons spelling out *26* twirling in the air as rollerskaters whipped by them. Rufus slept in our car during the party so he could be there, be part of the night.

For my thirtieth birthday, Daniel turned our backyard into a movie theater. A projector broadcast my favorite movies, starting with *Dirty Dancing*, onto a sheet on our fence. Daniel had threaded string lights above us, and laid out pillows and blankets and chairs below us. He popped popcorn and served it in paper bags, and invited our friends and their dogs and babies. We sat on a blanket surrounded by everything I loved, and I thought, *someone else knows me better than I do*. Until I saw all of it, I couldn't have imagined this on my own.

He loved me best on birthdays, and when he had some kind of project to work on. He was a hobbyist. There were the welding classes, motorcycle rebuild, skateboard stencils, pickling, bourbon infusions, surfing, the '73 Chevy named Bessie, Kundalini yoga, cigar box banjos, the flea market stall, Spanish lessons, furniture making, and others that I can't even remember anymore. He needed these things. His hands had to move, his mind had to toil, he needed something that I couldn't be part of. I actually loved that about him: a man with so many different interests. But, like all of it, it exhausted me by the end. The hundreds of dollars it always required to get going on a project or hobby, the classes that were always on weekends, the hours of monologues of him talking about the new thing, when my eyes glossed over and I found it harder and harder to pay attention. Our house became littered with his former projects. And I am now one of them, in the house that was one of his hobbies, with the hairpin coffee table he built, his guitar in the corner, and a tub of clothes to sell in his flea market stall in the closet.

TWO

Leo

I'm disoriented in space and time when he looks at me, smiles and introduces himself. I don't recognize the strange quiet rasp my voice takes on as I utter "I'm from California," when he asks if I work at the company whose building we're on the roof of for an end of summer party.

I'm in New York, on a long-planned trip for a friend's wedding. But I know I've also come to see my friends here for the last time. I know the life I've found myself in isn't one that can sustain. I'll celebrate my friends' love, the first thing I've felt genuine joy for in so long, I'll hug them each one last time, and I'll tell them I love them, so they never have to wonder, and then my intentional recklessness can finally take me.

But now I'm in the gaze of Leo. The life I've found myself in begins to feel far away as I nervously avert his eyes, but take in everything peripherally—his heavenly face, the length of his tall body, his fraying denim jacket, the grip of his hands on his drink. Every spot on my body that he stares at heats up under the bore of his eyes: first my throat, then my breasts as his gaze travels, lazily, greedily, unselfconsciously, down my body. I'm touching his hand before I realize what I'm doing. He looks at me and tilts his head curiously.

"I'm sorry!" I nervously laugh, knowing I'm

turning bright red, and he smiles.

"Are you genuinely apologizing right now? Come on, California." He touches my hand with no apology. We take refuge from the windy balcony and find some chairs inside, where our mutual friend Kiki and I talk about a woman we used to know. I try to include Leo in the conversation by explaining that this woman still hasn't responded to my email telling her Daniel left me.

"So my husband and I are separated," I start.

"YES!" shouts Leo, and he jumps off of his chair so vigorously, it clatters and falls behind him.

"Leo!" Kiki shouts at him, mortified, but Leo and I barely hear her. We're smiling so furiously at each other that I don't remember to tell him the rest of my story. He lights my cigarette, then takes it out of my mouth and brings it to his lips.

More than once, I've looked the right way at the right time. With my grief body, platinum hair, translucently pale skin, meeting Leo was the time that mattered the most. My immediate intrigue in him made me abandon my recklessness and resume my life with care, caution, and intention.

I'm mid-first kiss with Leo, now at our third bar of the night. I don't know how the kiss started. We've been tasked with getting drinks for our group, but I need to touch him again, and I need more than his hand this time. We'd sat next to each other at dinner, our elbows in a constant, slow graze as we sipped oysters from their shells and dug out the meat of lobster claws. A current originating in my left elbow slowly awakened my body. Now his fingertips press into my hips, my hands cling to his shoulder blades and tug his hair. Our bartender, an acquaintance of Leo's, clears his throat with a smile and points to our drinks ready and waiting for us on the bar. I excuse myself, walk carefully to the bathroom, lock the door, lay down on my coat, and faint on top of it. When I come back into consciousness, I splash water on my face, which is now a true ghostly white, shake out my coat, and walk back to our table.

"I'm wildly attracted to pale women," Leo would later tell me. My fainting gene, at long last, has served a purpose. Now that the seal has been broken between us, a few obligatory sips of our drinks feel endless as we wait to get back to each other. Leo presents the idea that we'll go to the bathroom together for a bump or two of coke. Leo locks the door and lifts me onto the sink, then takes a step back to look at me. He shakes his head.

"Your husband is an idiot." He tugs my hair back and licks my neck and the tops of my breasts, peeking out from my dress. "You're so fucking beautiful," he kisses the right words into my lips. He grazes his hands up my thighs to lift my dress, strokes me with his thumb, then raises his thumb to his mouth to taste me.

"Come home with me. We don't have to fuck, but I'm definitely going down on you." He holds my head at a tilt by grasping my hair, saying this to me staring straight in my eyes. When he says it, I know I want to make him wait. I can replay this memory in my head a thousand times, and he'll grow as desperate for me as I feel for him. Waiting will guarantee that one night turns into many nights, because one night isn't what I need; I need a span of time.

"Just one more drink. One more bump," he pleads as I start to call a car, returning to our friends due to some angry door-knocking and a line of people waiting for the bathroom.

I go back to Kiki's apartment, and after almost a year of not being able to come, I come in seconds, my head pressing against the door in the bathroom as I chant Leo's name in a whisper.

Eurydice

The Guggenheim is installing a new exhibit and the rotunda is closed. I don't think I would have even noticed, and probably would have tripped through the caution tape roping it off, had the security guard not told me as I entered. I later find my ticket—I was charged half price for the inconvenience. There must have been a discussion about this, I must have chatted with a cashier, walked up a set of stairs.

Instead, I suddenly come into consciousness staring into a cornflower blue painting of Orpheus, drowned, his head and hair floating atop his lyre. I've wandered an exhibit filled with paintings of myths, mysticism, religion, hedonism, hung against red walls, cloaked in navy velvet curtains and couches, a replica and homage to an annual salon in Paris in the 1800s. The colors, textures and themes are in unabashed harmony with my night under Leo's grasp. I'm mercifully free of thought, and instead full of senses and instincts: I touch the velvet couches, inhale my unwashed hair, Leo still emanating from it. I let the blue of *The Death of Orpheus* by Jean Delville penetrate my eyes until they throb and tear. I tongue at a teardrop, savoring my own salt. I think of my friend, Jesse, who licks paintings in museums, a compulsion he hasn't been able to break. But I don't need to lick the painting—it already resides on my tongue, waking up tastebud by tastebud the longer I bore my eyes into it.

My lips wet, my eyes overcome, I move to a couch to breathe in the scent of Leo in my hair and revel. At this moment I realize I'm returning to the living: I'm Eurydice and I'm here to tell you that Orpheus brought me back from the dead.

I see a young girl, around seven years old, crouching in front of a painting, enraptured by the glowing halo of the young woman who is its subject, the sheep at her side staring up at her, the blue mountain and low lying fog, the yellowing grass. The girl kneels in front of the painting for ten minutes, almost in a bow. I don't move until she does, reluctantly, and only at her father's insistence.

This painted shepherdess would be Leo's and my daughter, the sheep would be our pets, our children would certainly have halos. I'm Eurydice, and Orpheus and I revive each other with music, blue paintings, red walls, velvet couches, and the fog and mountain envelop us under our children's halos. Only later do I realize I've forgotten the part of the myth where Eurydice dies again if Orpheus looks at her.

The colors restoring themselves into my vision are primary. I see blues and reds, I live within them, they live within me, my blue eyes and red blood. They're cast under the yellow of Leo, with his wild hair that makes his beaming face resemble the sun, rays of light blazing from it. He walked towards me on the rooftop during magic hour, shooting golden light back at the sun. Like opening a door to the daylight from a dark room, the unrelenting brightness sparked the floaters in my eyes into confetti, scattering and dancing in my vision. The primary colors have been restored first, in the natural order of things. Next will be greens and purples and oranges, *slowly, slowly*, I beg. Let me see in primary colors, in threes, just until my eyes adjust.

As I walk through Central Park after the museum, the wind against my face chills where the tear streaked down to my mouth. I imagine blue cornflower paint dripping from my eye to my lips, and that every stranger I walk by can see it. When I reach the other side of the park and catch my reflection in a shop window, I'm stunned to see no visible streak of blue. There's no tell on my exterior. How will they all know that I've been resurrected?

Lucky Penny

When I land back in California, Leo calls and says I need to fly back to New York as soon as possible. We need to embark on a weekend of drugs and fucking in the woods. I use my half of the unspent honeymoon money to book a cabin and rent a car, to run to upstate New York with a man I've spent 5 hours with. I ask Daniel for some MDMA, knowing he'll be able to get it from someone at the commune and he dutifully leaves it for me during one of his hikes into town. I come back from walking Ladybird and find it on my kitchen table in an envelope, which I immediately address to Leo and send across the country so it will be waiting for me. I've never once felt smug towards Daniel until this moment. *I will use your drugs and my half of the honeymoon money, though I should use it all, to be with a man who wants to be with me, who wants to take a love potion with me and dress me as a woodland nymph and touch my body that he thinks is magic.*

Leo and I arrive at the cabin at midnight, and we're so magnetized to each other that it takes us a comical amount of time and effort to bundle up, gather firewood, make drinks, and take the MDMA. We can't stop interrupting our tasks to kiss and tickle each other, and one of us has to push the other away each time to stay on course. Our lips and noses are red and buzzing, our eyes are dilated, we're cloaked in smoke from our distracted efforts to create a campfire from damp wood, and now we're here, on my honeymoon. We lie on a blanket next to the fire, drinking, smoking and staring at each other. The radio had told us there would be a meteor shower tonight, before we lost the FM signal on the drive. We see three meteors bolting electric white trails around us as we rub our fingers and faces against his scratchy flannel jacket.

"We need to make a fluffy nest," he says once the campfire dies. Every pillow and blanket goes into a careful circle in the living room, and we find candles and string lights in the cabinets. We sit facing each other, our legs and arms intertwined, our cheeks turning pink from the warmth of being inside and the tequila we're drinking from the smooth bottle we can't stop touching.

"I know I'm on drugs, but I'm in love with you," he says confidently, placing my hand on his heart. We moon at each other's eyes, giggling like we're getting away with something, rubbing our toes into the carpet, kissing and licking each other's mouths and faces.

A few days before I arrived back to him, each of our nerves began to show on the phone.

"Maybe you get here, spend a day with me, and realize you hate me," Leo had said.

"Or maybe you hate me," I countered. I truly couldn't see a life where I would be the one to make that distinction, to be the one to shut down the potential of loving and caring for someone. "I like that we don't know," I tell him, truthfully.

"Totally." I could hear his restored grin.

I never believed that hating each other could actually be a possibility. And now we're on my honeymoon, my husband is 3,000 miles away, and Leo and I are in love. It's not because of the effect of the MDMA, I'm sure of this. Why I know I love Leo is this: Daniel had wanted me to do various drugs with him for twelve years, and I always said no because I couldn't imagine him talking me off a ledge if something went wrong taking drugs together. I immediately trusted Leo to do so, and I even looked forward to being altered with him. I want to enter all of his dimensions and want him inside all of mine.

"I want to dance with you," Leo whispers as he chews my shoulder softly. We stand and stretch, and our hands dance as we can't stop holding and touching them to each other, and our forms and shapes move and shift and I'm so warm and full to the brim I start shedding my clothes.

"I can't see you naked yet," Leo protests, covering his eyes. "I can't see you naked yet," he says again, more urgently. We sit on the floor and rustle through my bag as he selects an outfit for me so we can venture to the line of trees we can see in the distance, the property demarcation creating a self-contained den for our new love.

After the tree line and trying to see more meteors but kissing too much to actually watch the sky, we

get in bed. Leo gets up again and again—to change
the music, bring grapes and tequila, move pillows
from our nest to the bed—until finally, we're slowly
taking off our clothes, and sighing, and gasping, and
staring at each other, and trying to catch up with our
senses. He grabs my hips, kisses them and breathes
me in.

"Fuck," he exhales, attacking my thighs, pin-
ning my wrists down next to them. He travels the
length of my body, my thigh to my neck to my ankle
to my ear.

My earring comes off in this new mouth. In
our altered state, Leo tucks it underneath his tongue
and slowly licks the ridges on my palate. He sucks
on the earring, then hands it back to me, and the metal feels so good on my fingertips. I picture the iron
entering my bloodstream and disappearing my ane-
mia, the blend of smooth silver and rough turquoise
from the small stud telling me which vein it's traveling through.

Now there's longer hair to pull, different limbs
under which to feel a bigger set of bones, an unchart-
ed terrain of moles and scars and head bumps to
memorize.

"I'm going to make you come every time you
close your eyes," he boasts.

By the time we settle into sleep, at 7am with
the sun rising, he has all but succeeded. Under the
blankets, our bodies cling to each other as we start
to surrender to our exhaustion and overstimulation.

"We can sleep, but I want your perfect pussy again soon," he says, sticking his index finger in my mouth.

Throughout the morning, our night, he jumps awake, kisses me frantically, moans into my mouth, chooses a different body part to stroke and lick. When we get out of bed at 1pm, we've barely slept, but I feel restored, rejuvenated, rested. My body is throbbing, crackling, screaming in colors and sounds—my resurrection is complete. When we finally leave bed he makes coffee and we sit in the grass, letting the sun revive us, rubbing each other's bare backs and smiling broadly at each other. There has never been, will never be shyness between us. He talks about our children being the perfect height, because I'm so short my feet can't touch the ground when I sit down, and he has to duck through doorways. "Your hips could give me two kids," he says through the cigarette hanging off his lips.

We drive to the closest town and walk by a park that has a gigantic Adirondack chair. We both immediately clamber into it and sit side by side in its absurd enormity. When he sticks his fingers through the hole in my jeans and pets my knee, I feel like I genuinely might come, right in the middle of the main street of this tiny town, with a fire truck parked in front of us. He knows how my body shakes already, and smirks proudly. I'm on another planet, and probably still on the MDMA. A police officer walks by, curious, slightly suspicious of the interlopers with ripped jeans and oily hair and cigarettes and the dirty boots at the end of Leo's long legs.

"Funny place to sit," he says to us, like our answer has the potential to imprison us.

"I had to come upstate to find a chair my size," Leo says, flirting with the officer. The cop laughs easily, high fives Leo, and very immediately loves him, just as I do, just as everyone does. Leo charms our way through town. The antique store is about to have an auction, and when we lament that we're leaving to get dinner with friends, the auctioneer tells Leo he'll order Chinese food delivery for us. He thinks Leo should stay. The cashier at the new bottle shop beams as Leo asks for a wine recommendation, thrilled at the chance to show his expertise to Leo and curate his evening. He gives Leo 20% off and offers drink tickets for the adjoining beer garden. He wants Leo to stay.

Leo is telling me his superstition. "If I pass a penny on the street I need to check if it's heads up. If I walk by without checking, it's assured bad luck."

"What if it's tails up?"

"No good. Leave it."

We eat steak off of a wood board with our hands at Kiki's new upstate weekend house. Leo and I are ravenous; the only thing we've consumed today is coffee. We both like the bloodiest, rarest pieces. When Kiki and her husband Sam run to the kitchen trying to find the moving box that has the forks, Leo and I attack each other and bite each other instead of the steak. Having had less to drink than Leo, I drive us back to our Den of Iniquity. We're in scant, un-populated land. I've never driven in such a degree of darkness.

The deer comes charging diagonally across the road from the right side and I swerve into the left lane to avoid it. The brakes scream instead of our mouths. The deer runs into the passenger's side, by the gas tank, and the stopped car wobbles side to side from the impact. Leo and I involuntarily clasp hands, our shared fist suspended in midair, and stare each other in our wild eyes. Once we ascertain that we're both OK, he grabs his flashlight, jumps out of the car, and walks so far I can't see the light anymore.

"I don't see it, but I can hear it breathing on the side of the road," he says when he finally returns. "It sounds angry." He shoves his tongue in my mouth, wet and meaty.

We wake each other up in the middle of the night for more. Grasp for each other every hour to try to eat each other alive. Fuck through the rain in the morning. In the daylight, we look at the car. There isn't a mark, not a single sign of the deer.

We sit at a restaurant on the river, get grits for the table, and feed each other Starbursts for our sore jaws before driving back to his apartment in Brooklyn. He teases my thighs and holds my hand over the gearshift as I drive. "We should pull over so I can go down on you" are his last words before falling asleep. I drive on, unsure of how to wake him up to prompt this request into reality.

His apartment has some ghosts on the walls and in the shelves—paintings, photos, and love letters. We all have these. Finally, he tilts me over onto the bed and honors his idea, now that he's well-rested. The more sounds we hear, the more words we speak, the more we sigh and growl.

There's a hectic, chaotic clash of pheromones at play that can't be denied. When Daniel takes his custody turn with Ladybird, she returns smelling of curry, a top note in his new cologne. I prefer this to his natural scent. After twelve years in its company, I do find it hard to disconnect when his scent infiltrates my olfactories. I roll on a dark amber-color musk that looks and smells and feels like my first night with Leo, when I was perched on a sink with my legs wrapped around him. After that night, I made sure to apply it under each breast, in the curve of my clavicle, my hips, the point where my thighs touch, all the places I know he'll inhale. I can't tell where it comes from when I smell the same scent on him. Maybe it's just his birth given scent. Maybe that's why we can't stop fucking each other: we smell like each other.

"Before you try it: I know it's good. You're allowed to say it and thank me for it once. One time." Leo is making me his famous eggplant parmesan, which I think might be famous because it's the only thing he knows how to make. I've spent the afternoon sitting next to the water with my childhood best friend Mary, the queer Episcopal priest, who tells me, "I'm so glad to see you with so much life in you." I'm shaky from drinking champagne with her during the day, the slippery oysters, the retelling of the weekend of drugs and fucking in the woods. Watching Leo go through his methodical process of slicing, stirring, layering, monitoring, makes my shakes go away.

In line at the grocery store, Leo and I had talked about what makes us cry.

Things that make Leo cry:
- Father/son relationships in movies and books.

Things that make me cry:
- Other people's feelings.

Things that make us both cry:
- Babies.
- How much we love our friends.

We talk about our friends the same way, and he's always writing love letters to his. We start to giggle when we realize that just talking about what makes us cry has made both of our eyes wet and shiny. Someone in line ahead of us drops a jar of pasta sauce on the floor, and we step around it while on the verge of tears, but never acknowledge it. I feel high from Mary's observation, the vibrant splattered sauce, the dinner, the shower Leo and I took together. I am full. I want to birth Leo's baby. I want to be Leo's father.

I memorize all the newness I'll bemoan missing in an unknown amount of time:

- The slope of his back.
- The force of his tongue.
- The hard grasp of his hands.
- The acrobatics of his sleep.
- The breadth of his shoulders.
- The way his whisper turns into a growl.
- And the only way I can respond is "yes."

"I got you a present," I whisper to Leo, straddling him. It's my last night in town during my woods-drugs-fucking visit, and I need it to be solidified with a tangible emblem.

"This is wildly unnecessary," he says, but he smiles and grabs it. My day of crawling the city has rewarded me with a deer hoof to present to him. It used to be an inkwell, and when I saw it in the dusty oddities shop, I thought it would be the perfect spot for his drugs. When he opens it, he smirks at our deer mishap we maybe both imagined, but maybe happened.

"It's perfect for my drugs."

Unborn

I return home to the cabin, and in the mail pile there's an envelope from a hotel in Chicago addressed to Daniel. He hasn't been by to pick up his mail in weeks, and there's an avalanche of envelopes constantly spilling over the counter. This envelope sits on the counter for days, until my curiosity catches up with me. It's a folio bill from a hotel. Daniel's name and her name are both on it—they had spent a week at a hotel together in Chicago, my place of refuge, my sanctuary city with no memories of him. Now it's not just him; it's them. He can't help but infiltrate everywhere that has felt like a home to me and make it his, with no room for me left in it. It's not the only hotel folio I receive for them. He hasn't changed his billing address on his credit card, so they all come to my house, which was our house. There's one for a vacation rental in Saratoga, the caboose of a formerly active train that can be rented. He also took our honeymoon with someone else.

At some point he tells me, "You can throw away mail that's obviously junk." He's still expecting me to sort and organize his life but not to know any of its details, like he's my teenage son. I picture the dynamic if we had had children—Daniel would get to be the soft touch, and I'd have been the disciplinarian.

The first time Daniel came inside me, it was after yet another of his indiscretions. It was nine years in, and I sobbed to him on transatlantic phone calls. When the tour ended and he came home, I considered, forgave, reconnected, re-established with him. We were in the middle of having sex—Daniel and I didn't fuck or make love anymore, we just had sex. He'd been home for a week and we'd gone through the stages and motions that we had so many times, and I accepted his apology and a few days later, accepted his body back into mine. I had already taken out my contacts and we were in our bed falling asleep when he started kissing me. In the middle of it, he held my shoulders and told me, "I want to come inside you." Without any vision correction, I could only see shapes and shadows. I said yes, because I thought it would feel like an apology, like a promise. It was so blurry, I couldn't see him.

The last time he came inside of me, it was our second night living in the cabin. He didn't look at me the whole time. When he was done and had come inside of me, he turned his back to me. I waited several minutes then tiptoed to the bathroom, the come dripping down my legs. I slowly moistened a hand towel under the faucet and cleaned my thighs. I sat down gingerly on the edge of the bathtub and sobbed silently, each sob forcing out more drips between my legs. Days later, I would learn I lost the war, because I didn't even know I was fighting in one. She had won; they had won. His coming inside of me was an exclamation point at the end.

That was the first month I missed my period, right after he had walked over the bridge. I desperately took pregnancy tests as I again wept on the edge of the bathtub. In my sickened state, I pleaded for a plus sign, for a second pink line, on each one. At least if I had our baby I wouldn't be alone. At least I'd still have part of him. At least I'd have someone. I realized, first with despair and eventually, much, much later, with relief, that I wasn't pregnant—my body was just shutting down from grief. Along with my period disappearing, my hair started to fall out, and my weight dropped so low strangers started looking at my body differently. I looked like a ghost, a ghoul—just white lines and dark shadows. My body's act of mercy on me was not impregnating me, but instead of viewing it as mercy I saw it as another betrayal that I was being denied my body's biological purpose.

At some point after Daniel moved out, we finally went through the shelf of children's books we'd collected for our future children that will remain unborn. This had become Daniel's hobby years before and we had a finely curated selection for our imagined future children, who had a list of names waiting for them too.

Daniel will be the best dad. He's so impatient, but he'll have so much patience for his kids. He'll prioritize them in a way he could never prioritize me. He'll kiss them on the lips and carry their lunch boxes and artwork to the car and ask them about their day. He'll be slow and steady with them. Sometimes he'll lose his patience with them, and it'll make them feel so disappointed in themselves. They'll want to impress their dad and make him proud. They'll draw on his skin, he'll draw on theirs. He'll rough house with them. He'll put Band-Aids on their scraped knees so tenderly. He'll worry about them, but he'll let them find their own way and not show too much concern when they fall. Their bottom lips will quiver, but they'll want to show him how tough they are, so they'll recover and climb the tree again. He'll teach them how to skateboard, how to draw, how to pay attention to things like rocks on the beach. He'll take them to cities, deserts, oceans, and they'll be comfortable in every terrain. He'll make them laugh when they're hungry and grumpy and don't know what kind of snack they want. He'll find them tiny, absurdly expensive clothes that will fit them perfectly for even just a week. His children will be artists and musicians. They won't be afraid of anything, just like their dad.

Now Daniel takes several of these books for her nieces, who he calls "our nieces," though he never called mine that. I begin to understand that being part of her family, and calling them "our nieces" is a price that he has begun to pay in exchange for the life he wants. Maybe that was what it would have taken for him to stay with me and live the life we planned, with me instead of with her. Sometimes I still despair that I never gave that to him, that I told him it was too soon when years ago, he had held my face, kissed me, and said, "Maybe I should put a baby in you right now," and that our list of names and stacks of children's books will never go to their intended recipients.

Protector

Two months after Rufus died, Daniel and I temporarily hosted a foster dog, to try to fill the hole, to see what our house felt like with three of us in it again. She was a 90-pound American Bulldog who had been used as a breeding dog and then dumped after birthing multiple litters of puppies who were taken away from her. Her motherhood showed all over her body, from her swollen mammaries to her puffy vagina to her worried brow. Her foster family, who needed our coverage while they traveled, had a six-month-old baby and the dog alerted the parents every time the baby cried. They nicknamed her "Nana," like the sheepdog from Peter Pan who looks after the children.

When we brought Nana home, she dutifully rose three times each night to check on us, trundled into our bedroom, raised herself on her front paws to lean over us in bed, sniffed our heads and listened to our sleep. Her nightly rounds included puffing up the comforter with her nose before we got in bed and escorting each of us to the bathroom, then standing guard at the door as we brushed our teeth. After two days with us, Nana grew listless and started herding us from room to room, always rounding up Daniel and me so she could keep an eye on us together. We took her for long walks, tried to show her how to chase after a tennis ball, and brought different toys to her, but her depression was tangible. Instead of playing with the toys, she wrapped her paws around them and held them to her teat while she slept.

We adored her, and Daniel wanted to adopt her permanently. He was someone who needed a dog in his life. But Nana was a mother, and although she'd been robbed of her children again and again, she couldn't bear to be stripped of her role as protector. She needed something smaller and more vulnerable than her to defend and raise. When her foster family returned from their trip we saw her with the six-month-old baby again, and Daniel understood why we couldn't keep her: Nana without the baby was me without Rufus. Just like I stayed up nights to take care of Rufus and keep him safe, Nana did the same to us. If we adopted her, Nana and I would both be awake all night, checking on each other.

Hunger

This new tongue gives me his fever from across the country. This has happened before—I absorb maladies and infections. Chances of susceptibility are high. I want to fuck our fevers out of each other and sleep in each other's pools of acrid, sickened sweat.

"This is one of the times I wish you had stayed," Leo says. It's a Sunday morning.

"Are you having a cozy lie-in?" I ask, imagining a morning together of being sweet and slow and still.

"I stayed up all night and can't fall asleep," he responds. I've missed the mark, but now I can hear the drugs in his voice. I'll take this version, too—salty and fast and restless.

"I would wear you right out," I tell him, replacing my sweetness with a purr.

"I'm very fucked up. You'd have to work hard for it." He sounds loopier now.

"I'm willing to put in the work," I tell him.

The last thing he says before we hang up rolls inside of me for weeks: "You have a hunger." The conversation makes me higher than he is. I do have a hunger, one that hadn't existed before I met him. Or maybe it just needed to be acknowledged for it to hum. I'm not used to being noticed like this. Leo has a habit of sharing his observations with the people to their faces. It can be off-putting for some, because sharing an unsolicited observation can violate the social contract.

On the first night we met, he asked, "So what went wrong in your marriage?" an hour after we'd exchanged names.

"My husband met someone else. Well, a lot of someone else's," I answered. I wasn't put off; I was relieved. Being treated with the magnitude of fragility I had been for the year prior made me believe I was fragile. Nobody asked me direct questions or brought up my failures. The burden was on me to raise them and do it in a way that assured I was on the other side, thriving, and not make the other party in the conversation uncomfortable. Leo was the first one to ask. He was the first person to look at me. "You have a hunger" reverberates inside of me.

"Your hips could give me two kids" was a loaded sentence, in many ways—in body, in maternity, in gender, in expectation, in tradition. But I had never considered my hips. I can only see them from two sides. When he said it, I realized that he knew my hips better than I did. He had looked at them, contemplated them, thought of the maternity of my anatomy in a way I hadn't. That he knew a part of my body better than I do makes me dizzy with intimacy. I finally have an observer, a witness.

I handwrite this and send it to Leo in the mail:

Dear Leo,

Never again will I hear Tom Waits without hearing you sing along, seeing visions of the shadows your shoulders cast on the walls, inhaling the scent of basil, my neck itching with the muscle memory of staring so far up to meet your face. Never again will my parched tongue beg for water at 2am without saving some to trickle from my mouth to yours. Never again will I drive through the trees without feeling your warm palms on my thighs, hearing the crunch of decaying leaves and bones under the tires, darting my eyes from side to side to watch for deer with a death wish. Never again will I clasp an earring to my left lobe without seeing it sparkle on your tongue.

He tells me he's received it and then doesn't mention it again. My letters go unread, unopened for months. But my envelopes with the drugs, he opens those right away.

Objectivity

When Leo told me he was in love with me on our second night together, he made this proclamation while we were on drugs.

He also said these things while on drugs:

The ice you made froze so fast.

We have four beers left.

Objectively, the ice did freeze remarkably fast. We did have exactly four beers in the fridge.

So, while under the influence of drugs, objective truths were spoken. If the drugs encouraged his proclamation, does this utterance of love deserve an asterisk?

Stool Sample

The word "husband" never felt native to my tongue. It felt like an intrusion, like someone else's word. Daniel called me his wife so easily, it seemed too effortless. He started introducing me as his wife when we first got engaged.

"But that's not true, not yet," I told him. He liked the word better than "fiancé." For me, "husband" never felt like the truth. It felt like a way to kill him.

"Why do you want to marry me?" I had asked when he proposed.

"I like the idea of you being my wife," he responded. I hated this answer.

"Husband" felt like a lie, but "ex-husband" came out of my mouth so easily.

Daniel used to track me around a room. Now I pay little attention as he boxes up his belongings, at my request. I throw out all the knick knacks that have cluttered my life, around which I've daintily dusted, for over a decade. I remember carrying his stool sample around in my purse, trying to find a FedEx drop box to send it to the gastroenterologist's lab. The unopened letters to Leo are a pleasant trade.

Ladybird

Ladybird came into our lives like this: a couple months after our attempt to take care of Nana but having her take care of us, Daniel's need for a dog reached fever pitch. I wasn't ready yet after the loss of Rufus, but Daniel was becoming more despondent, and his need mattered more to me. I went to the shelter and slowly walked cage by cage greeting each dog and reading their information cards. I wanted the feeling of when I first saw Rufus' photo, that instant connection, the visceral reaction before conscious thought, but feared I would never feel it about anyone again.

She was cowering in the corner of her cage, so small and frightened that at first I thought it was empty. Her information card said she was a three-year-old Shar Pei, her name was "Cookie," and she'd been surrendered by her owners. I felt the feeling.

The kennel volunteer I urgently flagged down told me Cookie had been left alone for ten hours per day and her owners didn't like that she couldn't hold her bladder for that long, so when animal control found her escaped from the backyard, the family didn't want her back.

She was terrified of people and wilted when anyone tried to put a leash on her at the shelter, so the volunteer had me sit inside Cookie's cage to meet her. I slipped inside the metal gate, sat down, and ignored her, as instructed. After twenty minutes, she approached to sniff me with her giant manatee nose. After forty-five minutes, she lay down next to me and fell asleep with her tail touching my thigh.

When I brought Daniel to the shelter to meet her the next day, she remembered me, then did the same slow warm up with him. Because she was still too scared to have a leash put around her neck, Daniel carried her to our car after we had signed the adoption paperwork. She took two steps inside our house and fell asleep for the next five hours. When she flopped onto her side, I saw that one of the ribs on her right side poked out the same way as mine—a single bone growth spurt that my body never caught up to—like she had inherited it from me.

Breathless

I feel irrepressibly compelled to play a specific song on the record player—"Breathless" by Nick Cave and the Bad Seeds. It sounds and feels like Leo. I can envision him walking through the woods to its beat, an easy smile on his glowing face, the sun picking up the reds and blondes in his mop of hair and beard.

Nick sings about Orpheus and Eurydice—that Orpheus' music was so stunningly beautiful that it caused the robins and the bluebells to stop their movement and instead move towards him, and fish even jumped out of water to hear it. My resurrection by Leo continues, in my woods, 3,000 miles away.

I look in the mirror and recognize a flash of myself, for a second. For the first time ever, my blue eyes look green. I had admonished Leo for saying my eyes were green, and opened them wide to stare at him, to show him their blue. "I'm getting green," he insisted. Now I'm seeing what he does. I explode out of the front door with Ladybird, and we run up the hill, my now-green eyes seeing their match in the trees and ferns as they blur by. We run and run until I can't take another step. I bend over at the waist, catching my breath. Ladybird steps her paw on top of my foot, leans up, and licks my face. We smile at each other and match each other's gallop all the way down the hill.

Canopy

I return to New York in winter. The way Leo says my name as he bucks through his orgasms makes me do it. On my first night back in town, he does lines of coke off my tits at my request. We fall asleep when it starts to get light out and the first snow of the season falls, and I picture our come covering the city: we created this wet, white canopy.

We spend some daylight awake—a long negotiation before we both finally get out of bed to walk a block for coffee. Our hair and dirty clothes and my braless breasts make our night and morning visible to the world. I crave forcing the image into strangers' minds of his tall body pounding my tiny one, my coffee mouth taking it in the back of my throat, him pulling my head up by my hair to make me catch my breath and wipe my gag reflex tears away.

I slowly get dressed to go to a party, counting bruises on my collarbone and nipples from his mouth and hands. My dress and hair only cover some of them, but the memories of how they got there will get me through this party. I always find a kind of pride in primal decorations. After the party, I return to my sublet drunk and find Leo still asleep in my bed, sweaty and boyish in a sweatshirt that has two raccoons on it. I turn the sweatshirt inside out as I peel it off his body. I know I can't come with those raccoon roadkill corpses in my mind.

Pleasure Paradox

Leo tells me he's a hedonist, with a tone of shame, as if I haven't become Caligula, Aristippus, Marie Antoinette reincarnated. Is it more hedonistic to procure your own pleasures, or to accept them from others for free? I will drink and eat and snort and swallow and suck anything offered to me, but I don't have the stamina or interest to find any of it myself. I'll stay awake as long as he keeps providing me with things that feel better than sleep. The loophole I've found in the pleasure paradox is accepting the pleasures offered and never pursuing them for myself.

We've spent two days watching movies in bed, on a projector that comes down from the ceiling in the middle of my sublet. I only use the projector when he's there, because I can't reach it on my own. We take turns getting up for necessities. I get moisturizer and feel his smile under my fingertips as I spread it across his cheekbones and down his nose. He walks down and back up the five flights of stairs to meet the delivery man for beer and food, his dealer for more coke for a New Year's party to which he will not invite me. I make us breakfast. He flips the fuse when I blow it. I refill our drinks.

I fall asleep lying on my stomach, waking for a moment when he settles in and falls asleep with his head in the dip of my back. It's the height of intimacy

of my life. More than a marriage. Neither of us moves
all night. We wake up in the same position, and he
kisses my spine.

Handfed

Leo takes a car through the snow to meet me at a hotel bar. His timing is unfortunate—a man who didn't believe me when I told him someone was coming to meet me is touching one of my tattoos.

"Lexi?" Leo asks. It's not a question. Or, it's not the question of verifying that it is me. I distract him with wine, because it's what I have, though I clumsily apologize, "I know you don't like wine." It's 1am and he's just come from a hellish day at work—the Prada account. We leave quickly and he wraps his coat around both of us in the snow as we wait for the car he called. When our ride is finally trundling along the Brooklyn-Queens Expressway on our way back to my place, he collapses with his head in my lap, instantly asleep. I take off his wool hat and gently scratch his scalp, then trace his profile with my index finger; the slope of his nose, his cupid's bow. When we reach my sublet, I put him in bed, untie his boots, and hand feed him a pupusa.

"I haven't eaten in ten hours." He sucks the salt off my finger gratefully, then kisses it onto my lips. I heat tortilla soup on the stove, and the layer of fat on top takes so long to dissolve, he's asleep again by the time I bring it to him.

I rarely sleep soundly with Leo, because his sleep is too captivating, his presence too exhilarating. Every time he rustles, he moans at me, twitching his perfect cock, holding my face, weaving his hands in mine and bringing them to his mouth to kiss and suck my fingers before falling asleep again. Tonight, he kisses my shoulder blade and smooths his hand down my body over and over, throws off the sheets and bends down to kiss my hips and ass, then comes up and licks my neck, whispers, "You have such a great ass." In the morning, he doesn't remember saying it, but he looks pleased with himself when I tell him.

I can fall asleep once he's awake and out of bed. He thuds around heel first, naked, starting a pot of coffee, making quiet morning machinations except for the songs he doesn't realize he's singing, my unintentional lullabies. Half of the time, he calls me once he gets to work because he's forgotten something: his glasses, his art proofs. I pretend I'm awake and out of bed, and jump on the train to deliver them. He's so grateful, I wish for him to forget something each time.

LCD

And then we dance, trade drugs with our tongues, lick mushrooms off a stranger's finger. I can only taste her skin, not even the mushrooms. A science slideshow is playing in my head: my taste buds under a microscope, colliding frantically with the oils and germs on her fingertip. Leo keeps calling her by the wrong name.

The next morning a massive bruise feathers across the left side of my torso from the balcony I leaned against all night, flirting with how easy it would be to fall off.

"I didn't do that, did I?" Leo grasps at it frantically, tenderly, when I stand in the light. I divert his attention to his hangover and pour him orange juice and coffee, open a window for a taste of cold air, rub his temples, and then I go to the bathroom and faint from my own hangover, behind the closed door so he won't worry.

Sexual Archives

It accidentally turns slow, intimate. The usual playful eye smolder becomes a soft, seeking sweep of our irises, the smirks turn into barely opened lips, the gasps transform into a quiet catch of breath at the turn of intuitions, rather than a response to a particularly strong thrust. He holds me on top, stills my body, and stares at me as he throbs inside of me, the surges almost meeting the back of my throat from the inside.

"Do you feel that? The throbbing," he whispers wet and warm into my mouth, as he cradles my face in his palms, then moves his grasp to my hips to renew our rhythms.

The next morning, the brightest light we've been in together sears in from the window. I see a mole on his neck I've never noticed, a patch of silver hair on his crown, some clogged pores on his cheeks. What does he see on me? The complex root system of stretch marks on my hips, the cellulite on my thighs I've had since puberty, most likely. The sun shows us too much of each other.

This doesn't fit into the unspoken agreement of simple hedonism we've come to, and it scares us back into our corners. We don't speak for three days. Equilibrium can only be restored by a period of alienation, by pushing the intimacy into the bowels of our memories.

When Leo turns down my invitation to the museum, I go by myself. My favorite piece in the exhibit is made up of piles of handwritten charts recording details of the artist's lovers' genitals, ejaculations, orgasmic expressions, and jobs. In my head, I fill in the blanks for the lovers I've had, just as I suspect everyone is doing as they look at it.

I ride the train immediately to Leo's apartment and suck his cock. Large, intense, active, strong, many words during and after, "oh fuck!," intensely sexual—unpredictably hot and cold emotions, art director.

"Can I come to your place later and fuck you?" Leo asks, holding my throat as my come-covered tongue plunges into his mouth. This is his admittedly brilliant way of turning down an invitation to meet my friends with me for a drink.

At 2am he isn't outside my front door where he said he'd be waiting. I find him on the stairwell, another tenant having let him inside. We no longer exist in public. We cease to have witnesses. He has them. I have them. But we, together, do not.

Sustenance

The last night I spend with Leo during my winter hibernation in New York is January 1st. I toil through the day cleaning my sublet, my fingertips peeling from the bleach I use to rid the place of our alcohol, coke, and come. He's been insisting on going out to dinner for my last night in town, but he opens the door with a blanket wrapped around his head and body, no lights on in his apartment, his hangover palpable. I know we won't go out. I know I'll need to revive him, and then he will sustain me.

He settles with his head in my lap, his long legs hanging over the edge of the couch. We watch kung fu movies on mute and tell each other about our separate New Year's Eves as I bottle feed him beer, massage his jaw, brush my fingertips against his bare skin, sweep my hair across his forearms, wake up his body with tiny touches.

"You witch!" He presses against me when he realizes what I've been doing, and that my spells have worked. He presses his erection against me and now I will sustain.

In the morning I wake up to him kissing every knuckle on every finger of my left hand. He's already late for work. We're falling all over each other and not looking at each other's faces and sweating into each other and gasping and growling and we know we're giving each other a memory but it's a memory we don't want because it's the last time and it's written in our skin and sweat and come that this is our final bow.

When he's in the shower and thinks I'm asleep, I see a pair of my jeans and a tank top I'd left at his apartment on the top shelf of his closet. He's folded them neatly, with care that shocks me, in stark contrast to his own piled and tossed clothes. As I get up to grab them, he starts singing in the shower. It's a low, mournful song I don't know. There's none of his usual boisterousness in today's song. I lower my hand like I was about to touch a hot stove and leave my clothes in his closet.

I wake up to him fully dressed and jostling my shoulder. It's not the tender hair petting he usually employs to slowly wake me up when he says goodbye.

"I'm heading out," he says too loudly. "Have a safe flight. Thanks for spending your last night here." It's formal and polite and I want none of it. I silently beg when he closes the door that he's forgotten something and will call me to bring something to his office, that this is not our embarrassing goodbye. I wait until I will almost miss my flight, but he hasn't forgotten anything.

He left a penny on his kitchen table, heads up. I don't know if it's for me, but I grab it as though it is and put it in my pocket to roll between my fingers for the six-hour flight back to California. Next to the penny is a Long Island Railroad train ticket, which I use to write my goodbye:

It was all so fun.

Love,
L

THREE

Foreign Territory

When the distancing starts, I don't even notice it. I'm in LA, because I've just returned from my month in New York and I can't bear being back in my house alone again. I drive to L.A. for a week and stay on my friend Nora's couch. I don't notice that Leo has started to disappear, the lack of phone calls, the quiet front from the east. I'm distracted by my friends, the sun, my favorite dance class, various parties, and weed home delivery. I cradle the newly pregnant bellies of my old friends, cooing at their abdomens so their babies will recognize my voice when they're born. I sit on floors cross-legged playing with toddlers who weren't born yet when I moved away, trying to make up for lost time. I hike up hills I used to have memorized, and smell the sun-baked dirt and dust I knew for seven years, Rufus or Ladybird tethered to me as I led them.

"I like the new you. You don't give a fuck," Nora laughs as she takes a photo of me simultaneously puffing on a joint and a cigarette, a glass of wine in my hand.

"It's so nice to be in a room and hear your voice again," my friend Ethan tells me and I have half-moons in my palms for the next hour from clenching my fists to stop myself from crying.

So there are more than enough distractions to not quite notice that Leo is removing himself. When

I return to my cabin, I send him a care package full of cookies, weed, feathers, shells, books, Brian Eno's creativity cards, a vintage Volvo ad. He says, "Thanks so much!" like I'm a cashier at a store. And then he becomes very quiet. I continue trying, but eventually the embarrassment of unanswered calls becomes too loud and I have to submit to the silence.

A storm rolls through Big Sur, causing landslides, fallen trees, and power outages. I'm again in a silent, freezing cabin, in shock at a man's sudden silence, just as I was in January last year. Another winter of discontent. Another span of silence where my days are filled with dog walks, dead animals appearing in my path, and trying to find the answers.

Leo isn't even there in my sleep. I think of him for so many hours during the day, my sleep tries to give me some respite. When I dream of mutilated hands and gouged eyes, I know that's Leo. He's in my hands and vision.

My body without Leo becomes a foreign territory, a frontier to conquer. I can't make myself come without thinking of him and calling his name out into my empty cabin, where it echoes off the walls and returns to me. For a while I forfeit and stop touching myself. I know it will only fuel my feeling of connection to him, and I know he's gone. But ignored by everyone, including myself, my body becomes so alert, so desperate for touch and release, that I succumb. I imagine it's his hands on me, and as I get close, my fingertips and toes begin to pulse with electric stabs.

As I come, my extremities burn, my orgasm causing
me pain. Tears come next. I can't control any of it:
coaxing an orgasm out of my body; my thoughts of
Leo while I do it; this sudden, strange pain, or the
letdown and the choked sobs.

From Across a Room

Daniel hikes out of Big Sur and into town. We've found a new, friendly rapport that ultimately proves to be temporary. We take Ladybird for a walk, sit on the beach watching a purple sunset with the supplies I've packed—a flask of tequila, a few bottles of beer, lime wedges, cigarettes. He spots an otter coasting by, close to the shore, grooming itself after eating a meal. I remember being on a walk together and seeing a family of deer, but not announcing it so that he could have the thrill of claiming them first.

Once the sun has gone down we return to the cabin, where I dish out the ginger carrot soup I'd made that morning. Daniel warms the bread—he always waits until it's perfect, something I get too impatient to do. We inhabit our natural rhythm for a moment without a conscious thought. It's the first time I don't want it. I suddenly can't wait for him to leave, wanting him out of my field of vision, out of what I now acknowledge is my home, not our home, though our shared belongings from our life together still fill it. Instead of feeling relieved that I'm ready for him to leave, I feel guilty. I could never have imagined wanting to exclude him from anything after so many years of protecting him. I don't want him to be left out.

I've never felt compelled to make a home for myself. I was compelled to make a home because I wanted to give it to Daniel. Now, I leave his towel on the rack closest to the shower, and I take the second towel rack, far across the bathroom. I leave up the two photos of him as a young child, looking mischievous and sad, that he hung on the walls before he left. I continue to buy his favorite foods at the grocery store. It takes me months to realize that I can come first. I can take the closest towel rack, and spare myself the frigid, wet, naked walk to the hook on the back of the bathroom door for mine. I can take down the photos from his childhood. I can stop buying his foods and make what I like instead. But I don't know what to hang in the empty spots on the walls. I don't know what to cook for myself. I don't know what I like anymore, or what I don't like, or what I am like. I realize I never knew these things—I just knew them in relation to him, to his preferences, to his personality, his experiences. After more than three decades on the planet, I still don't know what to put on my wall that I would like to look at every day. I spend hours roaming the aisles at the grocery store. I try to go to antique malls and thrift stores to find art for the walls. I can only imagine Daniel eating each item I put in the cart, can only see his responses to each frame I flip through. I consider that I need to be deprogrammed from him, from our lives together, from deferring to and concentrating on him, his comfort, his vitality. I admit to myself that I have no idea how to do that. That his influence, approval, and comfort have driven everything I've done for twelve years, and now I don't know where to start. I don't have a starting point for my own life, I simply have references to someone else's. But hadn't I built it for him? So wasn't that me, too, and what I like and how I am? Didn't I create this for us? None of it feels like mine anymore. I don't know where to start. I haven't looked another man in the eyes for twelve years without an opaque filter that we both can see, each staying on our respective side.

Daniel writes to me, during our temporary effort to become friends. *I can still feel your happiness or sadness from across a room. I do miss your friendship. I miss sharing my life with you. And maybe I don't know you, really, anymore. I don't know if it will hurt, or if we won't have anything to say to each other anymore.*

As I read this, I crouch next to the kitchen cupboard, my body heaving with sobs. This is where I come to cry. In a cabin of mostly windowed walls, this is the best place for privacy. If a neighbor drops by, I can sit here and they won't see me. The cupboard has been repainted so many times, it's thick with layers of pale pink. I fondle the edges of the cupboard. My favorite spot to touch is the drip of pink paint on the white handle. I can also feel Daniel's happiness or sadness from across a room, and it had never occurred to me that might cease to happen.

Run

The instinct of flight didn't come in time. The bird's brain told its body to try to run instead of fly but it couldn't run fast enough and now it's flattened to such a degree that I almost step on it. Its colors are divided by section: white underbelly, mottled brown and yellow back, yellow and brown on top of its wings, light gray on the underside, and a shock of red atop its head. Its beak is arched open perfectly in song.

The Nurse's Lament

Leo tells me I'm a giver and he's a taker, that he won't be able to stop taking from me, so I should stop giving to him. He calls me a nurturer. He's the first person to call me this. It's the most immediate, identifiable trait of mine that others see, but I had no idea despite my three decades inhabiting the role.

I consider the evidence.

Within two hours of meeting my Daniel I was sewing a hole in his pants. I told this story for twelve years. I wore it like a crown. I wanted everyone to hear the sweetness of when we met and he needed something and my helping hands were doing it for him before we even knew each other's last names.

When my friends' three-year-old daughter wakes up from her nap, I'm the first adult she sees when she walks out of her bedroom. She asks me to help her on the toilet. She runs to the kitchen to announce it to her parents: "She wiped my bottom!" They redden, embarrassed, before instructing her to thank me and telling me I didn't have to help. It didn't occur to me that I didn't have to do it. I'd been mortified that I wasn't thinking a step ahead to assist when she first stumbled into the bathroom.

For years I made nurturing my career. I took care of famous women, famous millionaires. They needed help with scheduling, picking up dry cleaning, pumping gas, grocery shopping, wrapping gifts, remembering to eat. They had access to everything in the world, but what they actually needed was a comrade, a peanut gallery, a friend who couldn't leave until they were told. Years later, I still dream of assuaging their anxieties. I wake up wishing I could have done more for them, remembering when I couldn't shield them from their own self-esteem, their insular disadvantages, their incredibly specific circumstances.

The nurturers never become the nurtured. When we need it, it doesn't come. I need it now, but nobody knows what to do. They love to tell me how strong I am, as though staying alive is so brave. If I choose the alternative, does that make me weak or scared or whatever the opposite is of brave? But there is no choice. I don't choose to be brave or strong. And I don't feel any of those traits I'm being assigned. Gravity pulls harder every day, though more often now it feels like I'm being pushed towards the ground instead of pulled.

When I had someone, people always asked how he was first before asking me, "How are you?" Now that I'm alone and have no partner for them to ask me about, they instead start conversations with "My coworker is getting divorced," as if it's the only way to relate to me anymore. As if it's the totality of who I am now. They skip the how-are-yous all together. Nobody wants to be near someone that makes them unsure of whether this could happen to them. If I mention Daniel they become visibly tense, like I should know we don't speak of the living dead.

Loneliness is a necessary alienation. I can't face anyone when I don't know what to tell them, admit what's happening, or say it out loud. And now days go by where the only human contact I have is with the ghost hands of neighbors waving as they drive past. The glare on the glass makes it impossible to see their faces. I crave smelling Ladybird's breath because it's the only scent that belongs to someone else.

Last night I dreamt a mountain lion stalked into a room I was lying down in, its tail whipping devilishly, erratically. It laid down behind me and put its head on my neck. I should have been scared, but I was so grateful to be touched that I didn't have any fear.

I feel others on my body in different places. It takes time for me to learn who it is. I feel Daniel in my sinuses. I feel Leo in my eyes, my breath, and my fingers. What good is my body if not a shrine to those I love? A vessel for their needs and desires, a sacrifice for their woes and pains. My body becomes a decorated tomb, with marks to, for, by, and because of those I've loved.

I receive gifts of bubble bath, creams and oils, spa gift cards. As though the creams and oils are a cure-all salve for more than wrinkles. I accept the gifts with performances of gratitude, dutifully carrying an open heart and mind as I use them. The massages end every single time with me in tears. My body, this shrine to those I love, can't accept this one-way touch, directed solely towards me. There's not an exchange, so it feels foreign and mistaken.

It's a dangerous hobby, keeping track of others. Knowing them better than they know themselves, better than you know yourself. Intellectually I know this: don't keep people as hobbies. Keep them as friends and lovers. Don't keep strange things, like a piece of rubber from the sole of Daniel's shoe that lives on my nightstand, or the list of things that make Leo do a little dance. Let some things happen without keeping a record. Without turning it into your possession.

Months after Daniel leaves, the cobbler at the shoe repair stand eventually asks, tenderly, "Not married anymore?" as he rings up my pair of boots he's fixed.

"Not anymore," I affirm, matching his tone. "How did you know?"

"You stopped bringing his shoes and belts to fix."

Don't fix their things. Let them fix their own things.

Sacred

I wake up tasting metal. Not the kind I tasted kissing Leo, that sweet and salty copper. This is a sinister steel, so potent I choke on it. When I lift my head to cough it out, I see a sad clown face on my pillow— my unwashed makeup, the black eyeliner smudged into pouty crying eyes and the red lipstick a wide, permanent frown on the white cotton. I get high and eat mint chip ice cream in bed. I cannot muster a care about the fat clustering in honeycombs on my thighs if Leo won't be around to grip it while he comes on my ass. The sugar makes the sides of my tongue zing but my throat, raw and restless, is soothed by the cold cream. Forgetting that the chocolate bar on top of the fridge is the weed chocolate, I eat more of it and am on another planet.

"You have alien eyes," Leo told me dreamily on our first night together in the woods, before slowly licking my eyelids, my third eye.

I turn to my dreams to find the answers. With my intuitions turning so strongly with silence and isolation, I think my subconscious must hold something, too. I dream that I'm staying in the same hotel as Leo, and I beg him to see me as I follow him through a maze of hallways and rooms. Finally he agrees to meet me, but I have to try to keep his attention while his ice cream cone melts, and I can't do it. In the next night's dream, Leo is fucking me in

the same hotel—one I've never seen in waking life—
and physically something feels wrong. It doesn't feel
like him, like us, it's sharp and painful. After, I realize
he's fucked me with Daniel's dick.

I learn through a friend that Leo is in California. When I look up the hotel he's staying in, it
looks precisely like the one I've been dreaming about
for two nights. My dreams hold some answers, but
they're answers I don't want, so I don't believe them.

When I decide to stop believing my dreams, I
resume walking for miles. I find three pennies in the
woods, all heads up. My back seers in pain, needing
to crack in a spot where there are no bones beneath.
My left index finger and thumb twitch incessantly.
Below it all, brewing in the caverns of my body, is a
sharp and shocking cramp in my vagina. I've never
felt this pain before, and it sends me to the ground,
to my knees.

Leo was the last person there. I want to seal
him inside of me with gold jewelry and scarabs, everything that needs to be kept sacred. *Seal yourself like
a sacred tomb with him inside, so he doesn't escape, and so
nobody trespasses into his holiness inside of you.*

Unsurfaced

I fly back to New York in March on a red-eye. Leo and I haven't spoken in months. I expect he'll do one of two things: make me come or make me cry.

The first thing I do when I land is get a tarot reading at my favorite bookstore in Brooklyn for guidance, a cheat sheet into what this trip might bring. The first card she pulls shows a woman posturing heroically over a sword that has slain a man.

"You need to turn your fire to you. You're depleted because you don't feed your fire to yourself. Only to others." She turns another card. "Your little feet are running in every direction where they can find a place to be numb." She turns over the last card. "The pheromones. You're being guided strongly by pheromones. Get out of your house. Walk by the ocean. Practice some discipline."

I sit in Kiki's expensive chair, paralyzed, for days. The intricately woven ropes cradle me in the places Leo's gloriously domineering hands should be. He doesn't make me come. We don't see each other. He responds evasively to my drink invitation before his ultimate silence. My body reacts in an outpouring of maladies: an ulcer permeates the waterline of my right eye; an unexplained hole opens on my thumbprint; my head and chest are ravaged by a cold, and the first knuckle of my left index finger blossoms an unexplained, horrifyingly iris bruise, with a hard bump on the bone. I remember a bible cyst on my wrist years ago that went away after I insisted Daniel whack it with a book. I try to do the same with my finger. The pain knocks the wind out of me, enrages the bruise and bump.

"He's still in progress. He's not ready for you yet," Kiki tells me about Leo. I step on the plane back to California right foot first—my penny superstition. I remember the way Leo's heart beat so specifically, strongly, certainly, that it rattled the couch. I felt safe and protected in the tiny space he created for me in his bed, with his body sleeping diagonally, making a small triangle for me to sleep in. The triangle got smaller over time as he took more space, and my position became more fetal. By dawn, my legs were crunched and aching from being compressed and charley horses brewed constantly from deep inside my calf muscles, leaving me writhing in his bed. Now, I roll on his scent when I need to be brave—when I travel, when I'm forced to interact with people—all of the occasions where I reluctantly have to acknowledge I'm part of a society. I arm myself with him and it works. I wake up smelling of our shared sleep and am dismantled when he's not next to me, on top of me, inside of me.

My last night of thirty-three I drink gin and play with Ladybird, tossing her a ball, my socks, all of her favorite things. She tires before I do, and I get down on her bed and curl up with her, nuzzling her wrinkly head, playing with her floppy paws. I wake up an hour later, dry-mouthed, both of us overheated and blinking in confusion. I can think of worse ways to end this year than sleeping drunk in my dog's bed.

The next morning I cajole Birdie to wake up early, telling her, "It's Mama's birthday!" I watch her jowls flapping in the wind in my sideview mirror as I drive us to the sea. I'll spend the day there with the living being who's now the sole recipient of my love. She jumps and sprints in circles around me. We take turns chasing each other down to the tidepools. I gently touch pea-soup-green sea anemones and watch them retract into themselves. I spot a bright orange starfish, smaller than my palm. Ladybird bounds around on the rocks covered in mussels. "It's a free seafood buffet!" I tell her. But she just wants to chew on the shells, she doesn't even eat the meat inside. She tosses a piece of driftwood to herself around the beach, burying it and digging it back up. I must admit to myself I want to conjure a birthday call from Leo, I want him to be part of this year starting. But I know he doesn't even know my birthday, even though I intentionally showed him my hospital ID band in a picture I sent him so he would see it. And I know he won't surface today. He hasn't surfaced on a day that has no meaning, so to think he would surface today is out of the realm of possibility.

Sleep

But why do I keep looking for answers? In their actions and inactions they have told me clearly things that their conscious minds likely could not.

The first time Daniel cheated, ten years earlier, I knew it from his sleep. He stopped kissing my shoulder to say goodnight, like he had usually done every night. A storied sleeptalker, he uttered another woman's name in the middle of the night, but clear as day. The first name on what would become a list of names over our twelve years together, a mental list I didn't want to keep, but that wouldn't leave my mind, a list that would bias me against anyone I met with the same name.

In what was the last month we shared a bed together, Daniel had night sweats, which he'd never had before. We woke up slicked against each other, the sheets soaked. He blamed me, said I was a sweaty sleeper and became repulsed by the sour smell of our sheets. Each morning he would air out the bed in disgust, pointedly waving the sheets.

"It's not like that when I sleep alone," I insisted, hurt and mortified. He'd begun to spend the night at the commune once a week, blaming it on the scheduling and the long drive. The scent of our poisoned sleep began to permeate the nights.

Leo knew exactly how he wanted to sleep with me each night, moving my legs and his arms until we were tangled just the way he liked, one arm around my waist and the other holding my head as he kissed my hair until he fell asleep. Other times he would say "I need your lap," and nap on me while I gazed down at him. And twice, I got him wrapped around my lower body with his head on my lower back. As my month in the New York winter came to a close, he began pulling away from our tangle saying, "I'm warm, but I'll be back," before rolling over, where he stayed until his alarm rang, never coming back.

Room 33

As I put up with the atrocities of being alive each day, my scant buoyancy slowly empties out. By 4pm, my vision is forcibly overtaken by the image of the dead bird I tried to save on my welcome mat a few months ago. I made a bed for it, a hand towel in a shoebox, with the smelling salt of a Q-Tip dipped in brandy on its pillow. As soon as I picked up the bird, I realized its body was hollow and its eyes were missing. The outside of its body, every single feather, appeared intact. I feel like that empty dead bird after too many waking hours.

It took Leo fucking my organs back into me for me to open my eyes again. Pupils and irises inside my lids instead of shocked black holes.

Until I see him again, I can't take a deep breath and my ribs feel like they're going to break when I try. The more I can't get depth on a breath, the more I panic and need it. I try to ignore the pain, too tired and irritated to have another part of my body betraying me. This happens for weeks until I can no longer function through it.

By the time I reach the top of the hill, Ladybird is looking at me strangely because of the altered sounds of my breathing that neither of us has heard before. I finally submit and drive myself to the hospital. My body is engulfed in heat, my cheeks are electric red, my temperature and blood pressure are high. A nurse straps a face mask on me in case I'm contagious. I follow her to Room 33. The moment I've changed into the hospital gown, a crew of three women charge into the room, peel back the top of the gown without warning, and place stickers all over my chest to run an EKG. When I instinctively move to cover my breasts, one of them comments, "You uncomfortable with your shirt off? It's just us girls!" and I think of being naked at the pool with Daniel at the commune, unwillingly bare. An IV is ordered to inject the dye for a CAT scan, and when the nurse can't find a vein, she pokes so many times I faint. When I regain consciousness, one nurse is holding my legs up to get the blood back to my brain, while the other one is still poking at my arm, trying.

"The dye makes you feel like you've peed your pants, but it's just a feeling," the nurses and CAT scan technician all tell me. I wait for it, but I don't feel it. The nurse dramatically removes the heavy apron from my legs to reveal a dry lower half.

"I really thought I peed!" I lie, because I have to give them what they're expecting.

At the end of more tests, I'm diagnosed with pleurisy—inflammation of the lung tissues. The doctor tells me with a wry smile and shrug, "It gets worse when you breathe, so just try not to."

The Curse of Jewels

My wedding ring still sits in a box on the bookshelf in my bedroom, along with some other jewelry Daniel gave me before we got married: a silver and lapis ring he gave me for our first anniversary, a pair of diamond stud earrings for our ninth anniversary. None of it feels like mine, though I've worn them all thousands of times. I remember taking a photo of the lapis ring to send to my family—physical proof that someone outside of our sphere loved me.

I park outside of the pawn shop I've driven by for decades but have never actually noticed. Three men are behind the counter, watching the World Cup. They half-heartedly inspect the pieces with a magnifying glass, though one eye is trained on the TV as Chicharrito gets closer to the goal. The offer for the diamond ring and earrings is seventy-five dollars. I take it. With five fingerprints and a signature, I sell them for less than the man in front of me in line got for his leaf blower. As I package up the lapis ring that will unintentionally live in my purse for months to come, the three men erupt in applause. It's for Mexico, but I imagine it's for me.

In the months before Daniel left, he started wearing his wedding ring on his right middle finger because he'd lost weight and his skeletal hands refused to keep the band on any finger. But this was more truthful. He was no longer in our marriage. To have worn it on his left ring finger would have been a lie. It was a silent message, to me, every day.

I was wearing my wedding band the night I met Leo. As he wove his fingers through mine and held them above my head, against the mirror that my back was resting on in the bathroom, I could feel the wedding ring pressing into my fingers and his. Two days after I'd met Leo, I was in Chicago, in the hotel where Daniel had stayed with her when the receipt was mailed to my cabin. It wasn't intentional—my trip was for work, and the hotel had been booked for me. But it was there, in that hotel, maybe even in the same room where they had been, that I took off my wedding ring for the last time. I would no longer wish for this lie to be a truth on my hand. I took it off, put it in my toiletry bag, walked across the street to buy wine, and I held the bottle in my left hand, tapping my now ringless finger against it.

Ghost Phone

I read an article about a Japanese man who created a disconnected telephone booth to talk to his brother who had died in a tsunami. He calls it a wind telephone, because the words he speaks are carried by the wind. It's at the top of a hill and thousands of grievers visit it each year to speak to their loved ones. Daniel's old closet is empty, so I buy an old avocado green rotary phone and turn the closet into a wind telephone booth. The phone is avocado-green, and it has phone numbers written on its face for the police and paramedics. On top of the receiver is a phone number for a funeral home in Texas. I put a small couch in the booth, and wrap white string lights around the clothing rod. I place a potted succulent next to the phone, on top of a wooden tray.

The people I need to talk to are still alive but I can't speak to them directly. All of my ghosts are living. The first person I intend to call, two glasses of wine in, while the sun still hasn't quite set, is Leo. After weeks of setting up my phone booth to be just right, just like I imagined, I'm suddenly afraid to say out loud the things I want to say to him. I know, logically, that he won't hear them. In part, saying these things out loud makes me feel too self-conscious. But mostly, I want to keep these things precious inside of me, still operating under the delusion that I'll get to say them out loud to him, when I can touch his hands, his face, burrow in his beard as I speak. I still can't forfeit the idea that he'll surface.

Accidentally, I continue to refer to it and think of it as my "ghost phone" instead of my "wind phone." Actions continuing towards me instead of me carrying them out externally; a haunting instead of a confession.

Finally, I drink enough three-dollar wine to make the ghost call. The second I pick up the receiver there's a knock at my front door. It's a car full of French tourists who are lost and looking for their vacation rental. They swear in English and French, and light cigarettes on my stoop as I try to give them directions. The interruption provides my nerves with enough distraction to barrel into the booth and pick up the phone.

X-Ray

I wake up with an unquenchable desire to get an X-ray. I need to see my insides. I have an instinct that when I see them, clarity won't remain so elusive. There will be answers in my muscles, my tissue, my fat. My finger provides the means to this end. The bruising has subsided, but the bump hasn't. When I drink too much alcohol, it throbs so hotly it wakes me up from my sleeping pill stupor.

The urgent care practice is one I'd been to when I'd inherited Leo's fever and infections from across the country. I idly wonder if my knotted finger is from him, and imagine him sawing it off in a carpentry accident, or slicing it open as he punches through a window when his drunken storytelling becomes too exuberant. The exam room reeks of weed as soon as the doctor walks in. She's seventy and very clearly doesn't want to be here. She grabs my finger and presses the knot with no warning, rolls her eyes when I howl in pain.

"The X-ray technician's shift ended an hour ago. But this isn't broken. Come back in six weeks if it still hurts."

I'm stunned by the pain, speechless with sorrow. I still need to see my insides. I drive home, grab a bottle from the shelf and get in bed, too morose to continue. I can't move until I see the whites and blacks and grays and the slight tint of blue of my pathetic body glowing from the lightbox.

Curation

Stored memories of Leo keep me alive and I become reckless with them. I consume them with such desperation that I find myself miles away from my cabin, having gotten off track of my regular loop. Ladybird cocks her head at me inquisitively, game to trot by my side, but confused at a change in routine. I arrive late to everything for the first time in my life.

"We used to set a clock by you," various friends chide me, somewhat unnerved at my drastic change of habit.

I begin to set a timer; I'm allowed to think of Leo for five minutes, seven minutes, nine minutes, and sometimes for thirty minutes (only on weekends). These spans of time all feel too short, of course. Often, I'm so exhilarated bringing him to life in my mind that I can't settle into a specific scenario until the timer is about to ring. I change his location and, with it, his clothes—from standing under an awning in the rain wearing his favorite wool fisherman's sweater, to playing pool at a bar in his red plaid flannel that has holes in the elbows, to watching movies in bed, with no clothes at all, his long, bare legs hanging off the edge of the mattress.

With practice, the loop in my mind becomes a finely curated selection of memories alongside a collection of new fantasies. They become specifically placed and timed throughout the day. A wildcard memory of his voice saying a phrase can change the course of my day, render me paralytically morose, completely useless. There are certain memories, like the one of him charging across the four-foot gap between us because he needed to be closer to me, that I have to quell, again and again. I allow myself the memory of the kiss that followed. Anything that came before that is off limits, or I'll arrive at a social commitment as the dishes are being washed instead of during cocktails. I set a clock by him.

Thank You

Daniel tells me he's leaving the commune. He's moving to the East Coast to live with the woman from New Year's in another tiny coastal town, to be with another woman who lives right by her family, and start another life that's nothing like his has ever looked, that he will embody rapidly and entirely.

As he tells me his plans, he asks about Ladybird. We let the question hang in the air. I can only do this a little bit at a time. Daniel looks at me tenderly, understanding that I'll need to do this slowly, and I'm shocked that I've forgotten how gentle he can be—that used to be one of my favorite things about him. His unexpected softness dismantles the facade of courage I've been building in order to eventually part ways with Ladybird. I cry so violently picturing my life without her that capillaries burst around my eyes and Ladybird licks the mucus dripping out of my nose to try to comfort me. The next time Daniel comes by for his mail, I tell him if he wants a turn taking Ladybird to live with him, he can. I tell him to think about it.

A week later, I'm sitting at the kitchen table, watching the bluejays quibble on the branch of the oak tree. Ladybird is sleeping by the couch. I suddenly feel bereaved. I stand up, walk to her, and drop to my knees, holding her and sobbing into her fur. She doesn't startle, doesn't jump. She accepts this unprecedented affection and despair. She leans as I scratch each of her ears, and licks her chops as I kiss the wrinkles on her forehead, whispering "thank you" to her. Eventually I lean back against the couch, and she flops down on her side and begins to snore softly, her paws making tiny twitches.

That's when Daniel calls: he's going to take her with him to live by the sea again, on the other coast.

Restoration

The envelope comes in the mail with a stamp that says "Celebrate!" with a drawing of fireworks. My name and address were handwritten by me six months ago, as if to say, "you did this to yourself." The stamps Daniel and I had bought together the day we filed.

"The parties are restored to the status of single persons," the paper inside reads. I don't feel restored.

I feel a heat within me, holding this information. It begins to turn into the kind of heat that rises with an illness, and I realize I'm sweating at my temples and on my upper lip. I tell Daniel the dissolution is final. I've never used that word before, but it's the word that comes out.

"I owe you a champagne date," he responds. We had discussed marking this finalization with a bottle of champagne that had been given to us on our wedding day, to be drunk on our first wedding anniversary. Rufus had died in our arms 2 days before then, so the champagne is still unpopped.

Still, when he responds this way, it feels a little cruel. For now, the bottle is still on my bar shelf, and the "Celebrate!" envelope is still in my hand. I cower in bed for the rest of the night, unsure of what else to do.

But then my phone rings and it's Leo. For the first time in seventy-five days, it's Leo, and he calls

on this day, in this moment. He's spring cleaning and
found some of my things and he needs my address.
I wait and wait, but nothing from Leo ever arrives in
my mailbox.

Timber

The fire department issues an order to clear land, trim branches, and minimize the fuel for fires created by the drought. My landlady godmother hires someone to trim a few branches that are touching my house. I take Ladybird to the beach and to walk around town so we can both be spared the anxiety of hearing chainsaws all morning.

When we return, I stand, stunned, and I weep. The redwood by the front door, Tasha's "little sister," has been stripped bare. The oak that rose up to my office windows, in which I watched families of birds nest and feed, is now a stump. My treehouse hideaway is now a public performance space any time I walk into the living room or office, or when I lay on my porch bed on the deck. Neighbors begin shouting salutations at me from the street below every time they look up and see me. My house was one of heartbreak, but it was also my house of chosen hermitude and now that choice has been stripped away with the branches. I spend hours sitting in my ghost phone booth, or crouched by the pink cupboards, the only places to be out of sight.

I see Henry Miller's face at the fireplace, read his letters stored in the basement below, circle the drink rings on the windowsill with my finger and imagine which are his. I've held these connections to him before I even lived here, but I know they're imagined. I know I have no right to him, that we have no bearing on each other. Something about his Brooklyn accent and his bald head and books about traveling and fucking and living in these places I've lived make it hard to give him up, to forfeit this home where he spent so much time.

The trees have come down, and Ladybird is leaving. Why stay? Henry would have left. He would have decided that he got what he needed and it was time to go, but he would always send letters back here. I'll do the same. I start with a letter to my god-mother to tell her I'm leaving. After she reads it, she comes bounding down the path that connects our houses, wraps me in a hug, and reminds me that she was miserable when she lived here, too. Reminds me of the previous tenants—one who died of cancer, one who got divorced, one who kept the blinds closed for eight years and whose single piece of furniture was a couch, askew in the middle of the room. This is not a place of happiness for most people. I can box up my books, I can close the ghost phone booth, I can write about it from afar instead of from inside. I know I spent my time here trying harder, at everything, than I ever have.

First Breath

A week after the "Celebrate!" stamp, I sign up for an astrology reading and intuitive tattoo session. The astrologer will tell me everything I need to solve my life, and the artist will draw a design intuitively while listening to my reading. The guidance and the pain are two things I desperately require and covet.

The astrologer shows me a map of the sky from the night I was born.

"This is when you took your first breath. This is the moment you became your own person, and not part of another person," she says it like it should be a moment of pride, but it makes me feel inconsolable, incomplete.

The tattoo artist shows me her design: a circle with rays shooting out of it, two inverted triangles to show a two-way street in relationships, the whole thing surrounded by dots meant to symbolize my boundaries, but leaving gaps to flush out things that don't serve me. She has me pull an oracle card, and when I flip over the card I've chosen, it's Rose Quartz. *To be kind to myself, to move on from a painful situation, to believe that I am worthy of genuine love*, the card reads.

She handpokes the symbols into my arm. I believe in the delivery system of pain for truth, that the process of the needle and the ink being jabbed into my skin will reveal answers to me that I still crave.

It only takes a short amount of time, maybe fifteen minutes, and I want more. The message hasn't been driven into me forcefully enough for me to obey.

The design isn't what I expected—from the artist's previous work, I imagined eyes and moons. I'm grateful for the unexpected. It adorns my inner arm, where I see it every time I look down. Remember, remember.

It reminds me of something that I can't quite place. The longer I stare at it, the less it reminds me of something. I'm losing the association before I can hold it. Over the next few weeks, a few people, all men, comment that it looks like a rectum. That was it: an unabashedly puckering asshole.

The Telepathy of Motherhood

I can't say goodbye to Ladybird, so I pretend I'm just running an errand, and carry out the usual ritual of giving her a treat, telling her to be good and that I love her and I'll be back soon. I don't let myself think of her. I realize this is what Daniel must have done, mostly about her, but maybe also about me: *don't think of them.*

Except I know her and now he doesn't. He drives across the country with her in the backseat, and every day he has panicked questions for me that interrupt my practice of denial.

"She won't drink water, she hasn't pooped in three days, and she's doing a weird chattering thing with her teeth," he tells me.

"Put some chicken broth in her water, take three laps around a park with her on the leash and she'll poop, the chattering is because she's anxious of all the changes, let her sleep in bed with you in the motels at night, play with her and let her jump around and get some of the anxiety out of her body." I have the answers to all of these concerns. I know her funny, fuzzy, wrinkly body, its outsides and insides and neuroses, better than I know my own. I know from far away what she'll do and how to handle it.

When they arrive on the east coast, he reassures me that she's loving the beach, she's making dog friends.

"Has she been clingy since your road trip?" I ask.

"Oh yeah. Big time," he responds.

"Get her a new plushy toy for when you leave the house. She likes to chew on soft things when she's anxious."

As it gets closer to winter and the summer breeze becomes a punishing chill, he reports that he's tried to get her a series of dog sweaters to keep her warm, but can't find any to fit her body. I know her neck, her chest, the length of her body, and I send one that fits perfectly, addressed to her ℅ Daniel. I write a note, "I miss you so much, Birdie." I hope he reads it to her, that he tells her it's from me, but I'm not sure he'll actually do it. I begin to have a series of dreams where I'm giving birth to her, and I hope through the telepathy of motherhood, she knows what I'm saying to her.

Eulogy

Daniel says that we should write each other our memories from our thirteen years together.

What I remember:

When you wanted to watch Casablanca with me. We watched it and both cried. I remember you grabbing my hand and dancing with me in the middle of the street outside Left Bank Books in Seattle. Being Elvis and Priscilla Presley for Halloween. Eating under a full moon at a vegetarian restaurant, where a string of flowers broke above us and showered us with marigolds. The hummingbird that made a nest on the string lights in our backyard in LA and raised her two tiny babies in it. Making Christmas presents together: marmalade, vinyl bowls, hand salves. Seeing Low play at the Bowery Ballroom, and you insisted on wrapping your arms around me the entire show. Staying at the 29 Palms Inn in the desert, in a hot adobe house with cold tile floors. When you quit smoking, and each one of the bad dreams the nicotine patches gave you. You throwing treats in the air and Rufus catching them in his mouth. Your record was nineteen. Your thirtieth birthday, eating steak and pork chops at Deetjen's. Lying next to you in the flatbed of a stranger's truck in San Francisco, shooting down Van Ness, drunk and giggling. Nights at the Castro Theatre, sneaking in cookies from the bakery next door, and watching the piano player before the movies started. The roast chicken you made for Christmas dinner, that your sister raised, and the neighbor slaughtered and plucked. When the power went out in San Francisco and we watched the powerless city from our bay window and drank White Russians. Finding a piano on the street and pushing it two blocks to our house and all of a sudden we had a backyard piano. When you learned how to play "House of the Rising Sun" on guitar. The list you kept of movies I hadn't seen that you wanted me to see so I would understand your references. Climbing to the top of the hill behind the baseball field at Occidental College on the 4th of July and watching the war zone of Highland Park's illegal fireworks below. Years of talking through the shower curtain every night before bed. The first gift you ever gave me: a wrist compass from the Natural History Museum. Our weekend in Ojai, with Rufus, and a tub next to our bed, and the outdoor bookstore. Spending Christmas Eve in the Rain Room at LACMA. Having dinner at the Cachagua General Store, where a man played guitar in front of a painting of himself playing guitar. Going to the Broad Museum, and then to dinner at Yamashiro, where we celebrated your new job and our impending move to Big Sur, then cried about Rufus. All the notes and drawings we left for the other to find, sometimes on paper, and sometimes on a foggy bathroom mirror or dirty windshield. The photo of me wearing a bunny costume you had in your wallet for years. Getting each other the same Christmas present more than once. Some of the drinks in some of the bars in most of the cities and towns.

What he remembers:

    -You at 18, with rosy cheeks, red lips and a shy smile.

    -Sitting in an ice bath in Austin, wrecked by panic, and you taking me to the hospital.

    -Skittles separated by color.

    -Cold and unforgiving San Francisco nights.

    -Holding our dog's heart until I felt it stop beating, and then everything else around us stopped beating, too.

Doula

I buy the big box of condoms and unearth the lingerie that was optimistically bought and was never worn. I'm going to New York for another month, this time to find an apartment and sign a lease, and to fuck strangers. I will fuck both Daniel and Leo out of my system, I'll unseal the sacred tomb and release their curses from my body. It's summer now and I can walk outside and be surrounded by people, all of us with a thin sheen of sweat on our skin that gives a glimpse of what we look like in a postcoital haze. When I remember that now I have to look at people as I walk past them, after so many years of looking away because I didn't need to look at them, I'll look them in the eyes and bring them back to my sublet, a place where I can bring strangers, that I can pass off as my own, and where they'll never find me again after this one month; a place where I can be a different person. I pack nothing but black dresses to wear outside, and black lingerie to wear inside.

A week before my flight to New York, Leo calls again. It's 5am on a Sunday, 8am his time. Right as the phone rang, I'd been dreaming of a tumor in my eye, so I'm not surprised to be awakened by him calling. He's been up all night, has taken everything, and needs a drug doula to talk him down, so he thought of me. I can taste the cocaine and sweat that I hear in his voice, and he's so high I wonder if I'll hear him overdose. But he was right to think of me. I calm him down, a tenth of a second at a time, until his pace is that of just a few lines of coke, until I'm sure he's not going to foam at the mouth while I hear it bubbling. Then I hear his breathing change, and I hear the undeniable sound of his hand stroking his cock, and our phone call changes course.

I take orders from him. He tells me to get on all fours, and I don't know if I mean anything to him, but he means something to me, so I do. He tells me I'm a good girl after I spend an hour talking him to completion. He calls my name again and again and it's me and it's me and it's me, and his hoarse, drugged voice is calling my name, and this is how he takes care of me after I took care of him.

Jukebox

We haven't seen each other in six months, haven't spoken, aside from the phone sex, for most of that, and now Leo and I are going to meet at a bar, on a grossly humid August night. As always with him, I'm not even nervous. I choose a backless black dress, because my bra is stifling and sopping wet in the humidity. I roll his scent on me, for a bit of redundancy, for pheromonal verification.

He's at the bar, sitting up too straight on his stool, wearing the flannel with the holes in the elbows—it's too hot for him to be wearing this shirt, but I had told him once that it was my favorite. I see that he's been sitting here for the better part of a beer and a shot, and that he's nervous. His eyes are waiting on the door and when I walk in, he swivels on his bar stool to face me, smiles, and kisses me so easily, so casually, it's like we'd only parted ways that morning. His hair is a wild mop with tendrils stuck with sweat to his face, his cheeks are a deep pink, and his hands blissfully cold from cradling his beer. I'm so relieved to be looking at him again that I stare at him brazenly. When he notices, it's like I'm giving him permission to do the same, and he stares back at me. We sit at the bar laughing and drinking, but it's a different tenor than in the winter. The words I'd whispered into the ghost phone don't seem important anymore.

After a few drinks, we get quarters from the bartender for the jukebox and the pinball machine. But the pinball machine is broken, so we sit down in a booth next to it, and Leo puts his hand on the back of my neck and threads his fingers into my warm, damp hair, and then we leave before our songs even come on the jukebox.

Lease

My ankles swell and catch a tremble by the end of the day as I look at and apply for apartments. The heat, the pavement, the trudging up and down the stairs of walkup after walkup, make my feet and ankles look like they belong on a different body.

I find an apartment that's fine, around the corner from Kiki's apartment. The landlady, Maria, won't shake my hand and eyes me as she lights a new cigarette. I am far past needing or expecting warmth from anyone, let alone a landlady. She lives in the apartment upstairs, which makes me wary, but she seems quiet and uninterested in me. I send over statements for my life savings, which used to be double, but the California legal system halved it and now Daniel will use our house savings account for his new life, and apparently I will use it to beg my way into a lease on an apartment. Maria begrudgingly accepts me. It doesn't feel right to have to convince her, but this is New York. We set a date to sign the lease. As I walk to the lease-signing, I narrowly miss stepping on a mangled bird whose dead body is being pushed in perfect rectangles into a subway grate the more people step on it.

Safely

There's a divide between the Leo I met, the Leo of winter, the Leo who disappeared, and the Leo who's under my hands tonight. When I'm not with him I only remember the one I first met. It has been almost a year, but the first impression has lasted, despite the Leos to the contrary. I roll his right hand in mine, over and over, massaging his palms, his knuckles, what he calls his "ice cream scoop muscles," and I do it for so long he tells me, "You know I won't ever tell you to stop, so stop when you want to." But the freckle on top of his right hand that shows up in my dreams, that forces itself into my thoughts at the oddest times, is here in my hands, and why would I stop when its flesh is here?

He doesn't touch me, doesn't take off my top to watch my bouncing breasts like usual. He keeps his eyes closed, his hands above his head, and after shuddering through an orgasm, falls asleep. I wait for hours, for him to wake up, to feel his moans through my body, to surrender to that freckled hand. Instead, he slams his elbow against my head as he turns over, having forgotten completely that I'm here, or rather that he's here, in my bed, in my place. I rouse him and point to the condoms I'd set next to the bed. Instead, he pets my hair as he moves my head down, I swallow his come again, and he falls asleep again. The next morning, I realize he didn't touch me with his hands the whole night, except to move my head down.

"You're not even going to fuck me before you go to work?" I ask, unable to hide my incredulity as he gets dressed.

"Get home safely? Have a safe flight?" he asks me in response, like it's a promise I am obliged to make. I nod my head and turn away from him, get back under the covers to hide my face before he leaves.

"You're not going to tell me to get to work safely?" he prods.

"Be safe," I tell him, softening at him needing something from me and feeling protected by me.

He drops his motorcycle helmet, and I stifle a giggle as it rolls around oddly and away from him. After he leaves, I walk through McGolrick Park to get an iced coffee, without showering, and slowly suck the straw as I walk directionless, choosing right or left at each corner, while I smell his cock on my un-washed hands. By the time I eventually circle back to my sublet, the sucking and the scent have made me so wet, so ready to make myself come, that I drop my iced coffee as I fumble for my keys. The plastic cup rolls away from me, rolling unpredictably—just like Leo's motorcycle helmet. By the time I catch up with it, it has been stopped by the disembodied wing of a bird.

The Landlady

When I arrive back at my cabin, I continue boxing up what I realize will be the last house that Daniel and I set up together. I do it alone, for days, a torturous ride through our formerly shared life. I haul heavy, wide boxes to the post office to ship to my future self. I'm not surprised when I return to an email from Maria the landlady:

The apartment won't be ready. I'm sorry, I tried.

And another:

You can't ship your boxes here.

I just shipped ten boxes, all of my belongings in the world, to that address. I still get on my flight, because where else can I go? I land at midnight, tiptoe into Kiki's apartment, immediately knock over a camping cooler that clatters to the floor and whisper "Sorry" into the dark apartment. They wake up early to drive upstate. I wake up in their basement, alone, with three suitcases, and no apartment.

Maria continues to send me emails, always at 3am. They have no greeting and no sign-off. They start in the middle of an angry conversation, though I've said nothing, so she's just angry at me for existing. Another person to whom I have to convince my existence is not a burden. She finally gives me keys, after a tense, days-long communication through the rental broker. The apartment smells like old red wine and wood glue. The landlady sits in her third floor apartment chain-smoking all day, so the hallways permanently reek of old, stale cigarettes—so much that it's a relief when she lights a new one.

Five days into my lease, none of my packages have arrived. I shipped them ten days ago. I receive postal service slips, but no packages. I haven't left the apartment during waking hours and can't understand why nothing is coming. I order some necessities from Amazon—a tea kettle, some sheets. When the box arrives, Maria is at the front door, rejecting the delivery. Now I understand why none of my things have arrived.

I've spent days in the apartment with her on the other side of the wall, waiting for me to do something wrong, while I wait for her to do something right. I move back into Kiki's, where a coupe glass commits suicide, hurling itself across the kitchen, while I sit fifteen feet away. It scares the cat so much, he gets diarrhea. I frantically try to track down all of my missing packages. Some of them are located and I have them rerouted to Kiki's apartment, where I build a wall of boxes that her cats obsessively scratch all night. But most of the boxes are gone without a trace, lost in the ether of the postal system.

Dog Box

I have a place to stay for two more days. I pack a small bag with black clothes, three beers, and Rufus' ashes in a box to carry with me to the next place, though I don't know where that is. The two material things that matter anymore are my books and Rufus. The books are gone, victims of the landlady and the postal service. When I see a title in a used book store that was in my collection, I touch it, but it feels too soon, like cheating. And anyway, Rufus and I are on the run. We don't even have a place to rest our heads, let alone a place to rebuild a book collection thirty-four years in the making.

Rufus' ashes are in a wooden box, with a bronze plaque engraved with his name. They have a scent that I wish was his scent. When I close my eyes I can still feel his fur and hear the rhythm of his arthritic walk and the jangle of his collar. I can hear his sleep barks that sounded like chickens clucking underwater. I can feel his personality, his being. Instead of him, I place the box of dust next to my bed, where I keep a hand on it as I fall asleep.

I remember when Daniel and I took Rufus on a trip with us, and he ate a Fig Newton off the ground at a gas station as we filled up before starting the drive. Something about it didn't agree with his stomach, and he threw up in the backseat for the entire six-hour car ride. I was driving and I have no idea how we didn't die, because I kept my eyes on him in the rearview mirror the entire time. Now I go to sleep and wake up next to him in his box, and it's like we are both keeping our eyes on each other.

It makes perfect sense that when left by everyone and everything, when dispossessed of a home by every place and every person, when floating through space and frantically trying to grasp at a tether, a line, anything to anchor me, that a box of my dead dog's ashes is the one thing I have to hold on to. Just me and my dead animal. I find them and honor them all, but he's the one who honors me.

Exchange

Leo and I make a deal: I can stay at his place while he's working in Atlanta for ten days if I give his apartment a deep clean. If I come over now, before he leaves, and clean while he watches and drinks beer, if I give him a massage and make him come three times. I suggest the deal. He just tells me I can stay at his place, but I can't accept the kindness without a trade of some sort. I know my worth, so I insist on providing an entrance fee.

We hadn't spoken in a week until he called tonight. The last time we saw each other he was drunk and affectionate, soft and caring, and I think he hasn't spoken to me since then to dilute the intimacy. But tomorrow is his birthday, and I wonder if he doesn't want to wake up alone, if he wants someone to notice when the clock turns to midnight. Halfway to his apartment, I catch my reflection in the window of the train, and realize those thoughts aren't Leo, they're me; I'm the one who doesn't want to wake up alone on my birthday, who desperately wants someone to see it's midnight and celebrate my existence.

As I scrub the inside of his refrigerator on my knees, soap and water soaking the black dress I'd carefully chosen to wear here, I wonder if he's ever thought about me at all when I'm not right in front of him.

At midnight, I of course can't be stopped.

I abandon the crisper drawer I'm scrubbing in his kitchen sink and tiptoe towards his bedroom to find him. He's just hung up with work and is packing his suitcase, and I corner him.

"It's your birthday," I whisper.

"I know," he smiles shyly, and the expression of gratitude and joy on his face give me a new set of things to wonder about.

"Happy birthday," I say into his chest, muffled because he's enveloped me with his arms and is kissing the top of my head. It's the most innocent and boyish I've ever seen him—the effect of a birthday on a grown man.

He's trying to wind down enough from his late work night to want to fall asleep. We play cards and drink beer at his kitchen table, my bare legs stretching from my chair to his, where he can't stop touching and stroking them. I'll let him win our card game since it's his birthday, but not without flustering him a little. His shoulders begin to drop, his body relaxing.

After he wins three rounds, he lies down in bed, on his back with his head in my lap, holding on to my thighs and hips. I make soft circles around his closed eyes with my fingers, point arrows down his nose, charge his third eye with my electric love, kiss his lips upside down. His grasp on my hips tightens, our breathing gets heavier, the night is humid and everything gets warmer and blurrier.

"I want you to do that to my cock," he whispers, hands circling my neck. So I make soft circles on the head, point arrows up to the tip, charge his cock with my electric love, kiss it upside down.

I'm determined to make his entrance into his new year worthy of him, to give him so much pleasure it almost kills him, to make sure he never forgets me, to tie myself to his new year, and maybe most of all, to force a new memory on the song that's been playing on a loop—"Exchange," by Massive Attack. It's the song I wanted to play as I walked down the aisle with Daniel, so ethereal that he would always remember it as a dream, that his memory of me would be that I had wings. He vetoed the song, scrunched his nose at it and shook his head with no explanation when I suggested it. I haven't been able to listen to it since he left. But now I'm compelling a new meaning to it with Leo under my hands, my tongue, my breath.

Once he gets to Atlanta, he doesn't answer my calls. Somehow, though I know this pattern, I'm not expecting it. I remind him that I'm staying in his apartment, as though that's the key to him talking to me. Instead, he seems annoyed, too busy with work to acknowledge this as an intimacy. I lie in his bed without him and listen to "Exchange," which is a mistake. Now this is its memory.

I can choose one intimacy. I can speak with him, or I can stay in his apartment. I can sleep with him, or I can meet him for a drink. They can't coexist. I've been in his apartment for six days, and from the

South, the only dispatch I've received from him is the word "No," when I asked if he was surviving. Though I have no home, I'd choose the intimacy of more than one word over the intimacy of staying in his apartment, alone. I pour my anxiety into deep cleaning his place. My knees form rashes from the hours I spend on them, scrubbing every corner, accidentally kneeling in bleach as I bring the dirt and dullness to a sparkle. I stretch as high as I can, perched precariously on the top of a step stool, to wipe the dust and lint off the top of the blades of the ceiling fan. There's not a centimeter I haven't scrubbed by the end of the week.

I've touched every single thing that belongs to him. I've done it without looking, because I haven't been invited to look—just to clean. I let in the exterminator to do the monthly preventive spray for roaches. I accept packages from the postman. One of them is addressed to me ℅ Leo—some odds and ends I can't find at the store and order online. Seeing our names printed together to his address devastates me. Beneath the devastation is the smallest stomach whirl. His neighbors smile at me curiously in the hallway, and I rush out the front door before having to explain who I am to him. Who I am to him this week is a live-in maid while he's gone. A boarder. Who I am to him depends on the week, on the day. One night, on the roof of my winter sublet, he told me one of the guys we were playing pool with at the bar asked if I was his girlfriend. He told me his answer was "Ah..." with a head wobble.

"We should fuck a couple," he'd said the morning of his birthday, stroking my hair. "You're such a nurturer, you'd be the perfect swinger."

"How would it go?" I'd asked him.

"We'd hold hands while we each fuck other people."

All I heard is that he would hold my hand in front of someone.

When he's drunk, the intimacies can be doubled. He tells me about the life he actually wants, in the desert, in the middle of nowhere, a bartending job, time to read and tinker and be bored. Then he fucks me.

He tells me I'm not allowed to use the blanket, that he'll be my blanket, and orders me to wake him up when I'm cold and he'll cover me. I think he's joking, but when I wake up to get under the covers, he asks, with his eyes closed, "Where are you cold?" and entwines his legs with mine, or covers my hip with his glorious large hand. When I beg for the covers and tell him my whole body is cold, he covers every inch of my skin with his, kisses my hair, and tells me, "You're so fucking beautiful." Infinite intimacy. I live off of this memory. When I ask him a week later if he remembers being my blanket, he says, "That doesn't sound like me."

As I pace his apartment, I feel an anxious wave, and see something in my peripheral vision. I hold still, one foot barely touching the ground, and within seconds, a tiny mouse appears from under the oven. It skitters around the apartment, from the stove to the kitchen table.

"You have a kitchen mouse," I tell Leo on the phone, after he has returned and is in his apartment without me.

He groans.

"Herbert is just looking for food, or perhaps another mouse friend," I tell him.

"Herbert?" he asks, laughing.

"Yes, Herbert."

"Herbert is dead," Leo wails a week later.

"Did you set traps?" I ask. Leo reports his theory that Herbert ate some crumbs on the floor from an edible pot chocolate. He found Herbert dead, lying face down in the living room. Herbert's accidental drug overdose, instead of his planned death by trap, touches something deeply in Leo. He tells me he didn't pick up Herbert's body for two days, because he was too upset.

My curse of the dead animal has extended to Leo.

Limes

Leo is going on his great adventure. He and his motorcycle, and them alone, are going to Bozeman, or maybe they'll only make it as far as Marfa, or maybe they'll head all the way west, to LA. He needs to quit his job and he knows he won't do it unless he has a plan. He and his bike will spend three weeks finding where they'll settle, then he'll come back and pack up his apartment, the only place we exist, inside those four walls, and he'll move somewhere else. He'll be a carpenter or a bartender again, he'll do things with his hands, he'll read, and he'll have the luxury of being bored again. I can see this life clearly. I dream of him on his motorcycle, where he's happy and free. In those dreams, he sometimes crashes his bike. Sometimes just some road rash, other times with more permanent and devastating consequences. In that dream life, he always ends up at my doorstep and I cut wedges of lime for him to suck on, and he is healed, he comes back to life. He comes back to me.

When I was a child living in Mexico at nine years old I got sick to my stomach one morning. I vomited in the street—pink Pepto Bismol vomit trickling through the cobblestones. My dad took me to a restaurant around the corner, where they were setting up for the day, and he spoke to the cook. She raised her finger, "Ah!" and disappeared. She returned with a plate of lime wedges and held my cheek for one second to give me a sympathetic look directly in my eyes. Since then, limes have cured my ailments. And so they appear in my dreams where I can heal Leo.

The traumatic parts of those dreams resurface while I'm awake and I know I need to send him with a good luck charm. I know it has to be his superstition to keep him safe—a lucky penny. Frantic that I haven't found one after a few days of examining my change, I find a coin dealer in the Yellow Pages who tracks down a penny from Leo's birth year. I try to find someone who will drill a hole into it to make it into a keychain Leo can put on his motorcycle keychain, so any time he's riding he'll have luck and protection. So every time he's riding, he'll think of me. But nobody will drill a hole in it and I'm told with a sniff, "That's destroying government property" on more than one occasion. "It's just a penny," I plead each time.

I walk by an upscale jewelry store with three young, tattooed women working just inside the window. There are nothing but diamonds in the display cases, but something about this place makes me feel hopeful. A blonde woman with bangs asks how she can help me and I explain my situation.

"My friend is going on a solo motorcycle trip, and he's penny superstitious, and I wanted to send him off with a good luck charm," I say.

Then I look her in the eyes and hear myself say through my anxious, sweaty lips, "I'm obviously in love with him."

Her kind face cracks into a smile. "Let's see what we can do. Mark on the penny where you'd like the hole."

I carefully make a dot to the right of Abraham Lincoln's nose (a nose which I'd admired before, but compared to the perfect angles of Leo's nose, Honest Abe's is an extremely distant second), leaving the birth year easily visible. I slowly pace the store, looking at the jewelry I can never afford, but that I suddenly want to buy. I hear the metallic clatter of the drill on the penny, the satisfying crunch and whirr. She brings it over to me to inspect, and I ask her how much I owe her.

"Nothing. My boyfriend rides a motorcycle, too. Just tell him to be safe," she says, touching my elbow. Her kindness and kinship make me teary, and we both giggle as she sees the tears welling in my eyes while I thank her effusively.

I have a lucky penny made for Leo and another wish for his safety. I don't hear from him for days. I begin to wonder if I'll ever see him again.

Finally he invites me over to cook dinner, and in my excitement, I forget all about the penny, left behind on my desk at home. I whirl into his kitchen and roast chickpeas and sweet potatoes, chop cilantro and avocado, sprinkle sunflower seeds, singing and dancing while I cook. His eyes are on me the whole time, though he pretends he's working and not watching. At the end, I cut lime wedges. He sets the table, and as we sit down, he moves his chair closer to mine, at an odd angle, so our knees press into each other. We squeeze the lime wedges over our plates, and suck the cold, tangy juice off our dripping thumbs at the same time. It's a simple dinner, one I've made so many times, but it tastes better than any other time I've made it. He's grateful, wiggles his shoulders in a seated dance and kisses me halfway through dinner.

After we eat, we start to watch a movie, but we give up fifteen minutes in because Leo can't stop staring at me, stroking and smelling my hair, running his hands over my hips and breasts. I accidentally cooked him a love potion, just from uttering out loud to a stranger that I'm in love with him.

We wake up later, his hand in my hair, and he wants us both to guess the time. I guess 1am and he guesses 2:30am, but it's only midnight.

"We have so much time," he smiles, and digs his fingertips into my hips.

The next morning he leaves for work at 7am in a rush, in a racket, from a call he'd missed overnight. He kisses the back of my head and tells me to leave the key in the mailbox. I know. I know where the key goes. I know that even if we think we have so much time, we don't. I know that cooking him dinner and accidentally casting a love spell will give me weeks of silence. But he tasted like limes.

The Neighborhood

When I look at the next apartment, I ignore that it's a half-block from the first apartment Daniel and I moved into together, the place where we lived for three weeks before he cheated for the first time. I push it away and walk up the four flights of stairs to see this new apartment. It has a view of the same water tower that Daniel loved to photograph, only this view of it is better. I can see the water. Daniel read a study that said people who live by the water have higher levels of naturally occurring serotonin. The study may not have meant the East River, but I'll take what I can get.

I move into the apartment with my meager belongings—everything that didn't disappear from the crazy landlady's rejections, into the Dead Parcel Room of the USPS. Because the majority of my clothes and books are gone, the closets and shelves are barren.

"You have an entirely empty closet!" says Kiki, something nobody has ever been able to say to a New Yorker. The apartment is empty for months, though I try to fill it with things I find and like: nineteen plants I fret over so much that I overwater them and they all begin to die by drowning, a table with four taxidermied camel's legs, a thumb harp and pair of maracas I find for free on the sidewalk in front of the old Daniel apartment.

As I've been moving in, I've made and remade lists of ingredients to buy for a theoretical dinner I'll cook for Leo in my new apartment. Each day I think of a different, perfect menu to make for him. Maybe I'll make the lentil soup with coconut milk and warming spices, with sweet ginger muffins for dessert. No, I'll make guacamole, portobello fajitas, and Mexican hot chocolate. Or I can go with a citrus theme and make lemon caper chicken and almond-orange cake. My list changes every day, as I continue setting up my place.

It's when I hang the third piece of art that I suddenly know Leo will never come here. He'll never set foot in this apartment. He won't see this 1960s nude painting I got at a thrift store, adjust the frame on the wall when it's off-kilter, or comment on the midcentury breasts depicted in it. I can't come up with a perfect menu because I can't see him here. He'll never walk up the marble staircase and laugh a single grunt when he reaches the top floor out of breath, he'll never play with my hair as he stands behind me waiting for me to find my keys and unlock the door, he'll never sit on the yellow vinyl Costco stool in the kitchen that I bought for him to sit on and drink beer and taste sauces and batters off spoons while I cook.

When I see him, it's where we always exist: in his apartment. He asks me how the move is going and what thrifted treasures I've found, but he never offers to help, asks to see it, or even wants to know what street it's on. He's never been to a place I've lived—just the two sublets—but I know the mildew rings in his bathtub, the lint balls under the desk in his bedroom, even the drawer where he stuffs all of his empty, licked-clean cocaine bags.

I can see the Empire State Building from my window—something the new landlord didn't even point out, and I gasp on my first night here when I see it light up at dusk. Occasionally a heavy fog comes in between us and the skyline disappears entirely. I worry about her, the Empire State Building, but she always comes back into view. I don't know if I worry about a building because I'm a nurturer or because I'm a New Yorker. I just know that when I can't see her gray walls and shining windows, when I wonder if I'll be able to see what colors her lights will be tonight, I miss her and I hope that she's still standing.

Conjurer

As the silence stretches and consumes more days, my thoughts turn to Leo on his road trip, Leo in his new temporary home, Leo as a bartender or carpenter, all the people who will get to meet him, all of the lovers he'll seduce with a smile. Another man who needs to run away from his life so drastically as to make it unrecognizable that this seems the only solution: burning it all to the ground. When we met, when he lifted me onto the sink, when he breathed me in and kissed me, he repeated, "Your husband is an idiot." But now Leo is doing the same thing as Daniel. If Daniel's an idiot, then so is Leo. But I know that the idiot is me. I can't give up on the men who I have to convince to love me. I don't even try to give up. I double down, I fight harder, I pull out stops that will haunt me later. The village idiot.

Except.

I wake up at 6am and Leo is calling.

"Is today your trip?" I ask, as though I don't know, as though the date of his departure is not embedded in my brain.

"Yes...but I stayed up all night." His exhaustion and energy are battling in his voice. "Call a car?"

Of course I call a car. But I take my time getting ready, shaking off last night's sleeping pill. As I'm twisting the lucky penny onto its keychain to bring to him, he calls again.

"Would a séance bring Little Ghost into this world?" he asks, using my nickname. Hearing it from his mouth is endearing and infuriating. He is the true ghost, the one who haunts my every waking and sleeping moment. I tell him to light candles and chant for the little ghost to appear. When the car drops me at his door, his smile is the golden smile of magic hour that I saw when we first met.

"You conjured me," I tell him, and he looks like he almost believes it as he kisses me so furiously we both forget to breathe.

When we wake up the next afternoon, I bring the lucky penny to him and he's astonished. He says a quiet thank you, then puts the keyring on his thumb, pulls my body to his, and he falls asleep again facing me, his hand clutching my shoulder fiercely. This time, I memorize all of it: his eyelids, his beard, his collarbone, his scent mixed with the laundry detergent of his sheets, the taste on my tongue of the coffee he made, the sounds of sirens and his neighbor's backyard chickens, the feel of his grasp on me, of mine on him.

He has my penny to protect him, though I'll never know if he brings it with him and uses it for luck or if he thinks of me when he sees it as he turns the ignition on his bike. He has a loose plan of his route and the cities he wants to visit. He has my lists of places to go—a honky-tonk bar in Nashville, a light installation art piece in Austin, hot springs in Santa Fe, the Integratron for a sound bath in Joshua

Tree, a list of ghost towns, a book recommendation because I couldn't help myself, though I did stop myself from buying it for him. He has one less day for his trip because we spent the first day of it in his bed.

Can you be in love with someone and not even know what their handwriting looks like? Leo writes love letters to his friends, and though I've sent him letters, care packages, and surprise birthday cakes, he's never written one to me. I occasionally wonder if he even knows how to spell or pronounce my last name. The things I've sent him line his walls and shelves now, along with postcards and international airmail from other friends. He told me when he receives a letter, he goes to a cafe, orders a coffee, and reads the letter there. I imagine what ritual I would create were I to receive something from him. Reading it in front of others feels too intimate. I've never been able to finish reading a book in public—even with hours left on a plane or a train, I will leave the last three pages unread until I can read them in privacy. So a handwritten message from Leo would need to be honored the same way, but with more ceremony. I think of making an Old Fashioned—measuring the ingredients, stirring it to the rhythm of a love song in my head, spooning out a cherry from its sludgy sweet syrup, carving off a peel of orange rind. But I know I won't have the patience for this process when words from Leo await me on a page. Instead, a glass of champagne, or an exquisite, gold-flaked truffle, I think. But I never find out what the ceremony would be. A letter, a postcard, a note, his handwriting, his ink smudges, his tongue-licked stamp—none of it ever comes.

Unanswered

When I couldn't get the answers from the living, I turned to other venues. I developed my hobby of photographing dead animals, making everyone else uncomfortable. If they asked, I would tell them: because my body died, and I try to understand why it doesn't look like their dead bodies. I've examined all of those tiny mouse guts and tender raccoon hearts.

Some of the trees expunged their own limbs, tossed a branch at me during a storm, causing my heart to stutter and skip. They'd harass me by angrily firing a pine cone at my roof, so loudly it sounded like someone knocking on the door. They swayed and threatened me through the skylight. *Do it*, I sometimes begged.

Nor did I find the answers in the moon and its phases, nor the cosmos, though I tried to access them in different ways. Spells, tarot cards, and seeking out constellations whose stories felt like they resembled mine. The moon was so bright I didn't need to turn on the pathway lights to walk through the woods, which felt more like a threat than a comfort.

I beachcombed for sea glass and shells, and mollusks who the tide didn't carry back in. I fingered our words, birth dates and names in the sand, facing different directions—north south east west. A whale was smacking the ocean surface with its tail so loudly and in such a pattern that I could hear it before I rounded the corner to see the water. A man taking off his scuba gear told me the whale was playing, but I knew it was in distress.

For a while I found answers in Leo. And when he disappeared, my hunt turned to him instead of Daniel. I learned patience from him, to put in the time. I fall asleep thinking of the places I've found the answers: his arms, his shoulders, his lips, and the sounds that come out of them.

I have to face that the answers may not even lie in the hearts of those who have left.

Body

My blood pressure has been low for so many years that I have a disclaimer: "I'm a fainter." But now my blood pressure is surging. It's so high that every nurse and doctor who takes it shakes their stethoscope when they see the reading, convinced it's erroneous. How can this wisp of a human, five feet tall and a hundred pounds, have blood pressure so high? That they think their machinery is wrong instead of my body is among the highest compliments I can remember being given in my life.

The force inside my veins is too high to be contained. My blood is too stressed and my veins are too small to give my blood a proper course. The blood needs to explode outside of my body and towards another body that can accept it, that can host it. I chart my blood pressure and track it, and try to think of calming things when I'm taking a reading, but all of the things that used to make me feel calm—Daniel, Rufus, Ladybird, Leo—all make my pulse jump now, where I can hear it and feel it throbbing in my ears.

At the doctor's look of genuine concern, I finally submit and remove all of the risk factors. The alcohol, nicotine, drugs, paralytic hours on the couch, birth control pill, salt, caffeine, oversleeping, undersleeping. I only let my body have the wholest, purest foods, I only drink water. I leave what's left in the other bottles on the sidewalk for a brave soul to take a chance on a street swig. I throw out all the cigarettes, I don't even use the gum or the patch, I just stop. I only take the pills I'm supposed to, the ones that I imagine bubbling to my brain. I run for miles and miles, I pick up weights and put them back down again and again. My 25-year-old body would have noticed these changes. My 34-year-old body doesn't. Its constitution stays exactly the same, puffy belly and thighs, dry hair, bloodshot eyes, and still, the high blood pressure. None of these changes has altered the race track I have for my blood. It needs miles more of a course than I can give it.

Still more of my body begins to reject me when half of my bottom left incisor jumps out of my mouth and falls into the sink. I stand, stunned, staring at this off-white chunk lying matter-of-factly next to the drain. I stare at my mouth in the mirror. The tooth has broken off horizontally, and has left a single spike daggering upwards, a sword being held to the sky. I can't get a dentist appointment for two days, and by then my tongue is shredded and bleeding, because I can't stop touching my suicidal tooth with my tongue. I poke at it ceaselessly. The dentist doesn't immediately file off the dagger, which he acknowledges by asking, "Couldn't stop with your tongue, huh?" Before filing it down, he takes X-rays of my mouth for twenty minutes. I poke my tongue at the dagger the whole time, reminding myself that X-rays are what I wanted. But for some reason, X-rays of my teeth don't satisfy what I'd wanted to see. He creates

a new half-tooth for me, and when he shines the UV
ray light in my mouth to harden the liquid, I think
I'm in the sun. It's the first time I've felt warm since
Leo left on his motorcycle trip.

Laundry in Public

The first time I go to the laundromat a block away from my new apartment, I'm drunk. I think this will quell the newly sprung embarrassment of being alive in public. The thought of becoming acquainted with the washing machines and dryers that are new to me, in front of strangers, necessitates a numbing. When I get to the laundromat, I'm relieved they have laundry cards and I won't have to use the change machine. The oppressive metal clanging of a change machine is far too much noise than I feel permitted to bring into a public place.

After I start my laundry, I sit down next to a chair being used by a small, white dog wearing a blue vest. When I sit down, the dog whines at me, louder and louder as the minutes pass, until it's howling while staring me in the eyes.

I see in my reflection in the window that the tequila turned my nose bright red.

Because I'm drunk the first time I come to the laundromat, every later time I go, I feel like I'm in an altered state. A strange universe where everything is blue and blurry. Every time I leave it, I can't remember what I did to pass the time while I was there. I can't remember if it was full of people or if I was alone.

Return

Oh, come back!

Come back. What would it take? If I make small adjustments to become the right one, do things the right way. If I just remember to burn some incense before the musty smell from the used leather couch sifts out again. If I remove all of my tattoos and reclaim my pure skin. I can create a new, fresh canvas just for you. You can draw on it, you can paint me with come and spit. I'll keep it pure and ready for you.

Come back. I'll whittle my body down to where it was when we met, my waist so tiny your hands wrapped all the way around it. I'll keep my large derrière that you loved holding handfuls of in the middle of the night, in the kitchen, at the bar. I'll be more decisive so you won't get frustrated when I defer to you about where to eat or how to spend our Sunday. I'll wake you up with your cock in my mouth like I always planned, but you always beat me to it with your fingers or head between my legs as I came into consciousness, warm and wet and so newly awake. I'll fuck you before we've uttered a word, before the world has done with us what it will. I'll keep my fingers and toes painted, so you see flashes of your favorite color throughout the day to keep your optic nerve satisfied.

Come back. I'll see my friends and stay out of

the house more so you have time to be alone, have time to miss me. I'll smirk instead of answering out loud so I don't talk too much, so your eyes don't glaze over when I take too long telling stories. I'll save my words for whispering into your ear and comforting you when you've had a bad day. I'll learn to make your perfect martini. I'll create beautiful plates of food for you that deserve to enter your holy mouth. I'll have my weak ankle fixed so I can dance again, just for you. I'll watch the kung fu movies you love, I'll eat the whole burger because you hate to waste food, I'll answer the door when the food is delivered so you don't have to get up. I'll fit in the cracks and you can stretch your long body over the couch and bed and take up all the space.

Come back. I'll meet your friends and learn everything about them, I'll remember their birthdays, celebrate their new babies, watch their plays with bouquets of flowers in my lap to give them after the curtain closes. I'll never raise my flag of jealousy when you ignore me at a party to flirt with one of them, but I will make you come extra hard when we get home so you know I noticed. I'll turn on a stranger while you watch and I'll hear that you mean it when you growl "this pussy is mine" as you fuck me against the bathroom door in the bar. I'll read out loud to you and you won't have to squint your wearied eyes at the end of the day. I'll massage your tired shoulders, your lower back, your heavy head when you're sick. I'll never stop delivering soup and honey to your door. I'll get you drugs when you want a night out to forget, I'll stay awake until you submit to sleep, I'll watch your sleep and protect it.

Come back. I'll have your children, my uterus will stretch as large as it needs to be to grow and hold your babies. You can fuck twins into me. I'll grow a placenta for them, and when I birth them, we'll eat the placenta because we created it together and to eat one of your organs might satisfy my hunger for you without eating our young. I'll prove you right about my hips. I'll get the extra stitch. I'll feed you from my breasts, along with our babies. I'll teach them how to read, how to be good people, how to stand up against injustices, how to dance. I'll still call you "Daddy."

Come back. I'll outlive you so you don't have to be lonely, so you have someone to take care of you. I'll be your hands, or ears, or eyes, or whatever function goes first. I'll spread your ashes where you ask. All the places you traveled—India, Vietnam, St. Catherine's Island in Wales. Before they cremate you, I'll demand they leave me three of your bones: a rib, from which I must have been created, and your smallest and largest bones. The smallness of your stapes, from your ear, which I'll roll in my fingers until I know it. The length of your femur, which I will try to wrap my fingers around, and remember the warmth of your thighs that used to encase it. I'll place them on your shelf of precious things, next to the ostrich egg. I'll eat one single tongue-full of your ashes and you can see my insides and your own farewell tour. I can taste you in a way nobody else has and I can choke on you again. I'll snort you like we used to snort coke off each other's bodies. I'll change the eye color on my driver's license, to the way you saw them, because under your golden light, you turned my blue eyes green.

Come back to me.

Or I can come to you.

Whichever is easier for you.

Lights

I can't imagine being longed for because I would never leave someone wanting. I can't imagine if this love was returned, can't imagine him replacing the light bulbs in my lamps like I did for him. To be cared for the way I care for him would tip us off our axis. I save the burnt-out bulbs to remind myself: you don't actually want this. Stepping down to meet someone halfway would be a compromise I couldn't agree to, a sacrifice I can't bear. I've never been important, but I would like to be taken seriously.

I perform love frantically, a step ahead of what's asked for. Now I know not to do this, but I don't know how to stop my nature. Natural selection will leave me behind for not performing love correctly and never evolving past it. I just want to be a joy and not a burden.

On Valentine's Day, two years after Daniel left, I look out my apartment window to check on the Empire State Building. Her lights tonight are bright red, and they're pulsing to show a heartbeat: a sonogram telling me that I will continue as a mother to all and a lover to none.

EPILOGUE

"She barked at the first customer of the day and then fell asleep," Daniel texts me about Ladybird from the used bookstore he now owns. "She's snoring like a lumberjack in the Architecture section."

He sends me these missives occasionally. The last update was that she had accidentally swallowed, and then threw back up, a cat toy that belonged to his wife Georgina's cat. That one came with a video narrated by her - his wife, Georgina - asking, "Are you OK, Bird? Are you OK, puppy?" in a sweet and silly melody.

I can finally make myself say Georgina's name. She loves Ladybird like I do. When I think about how grateful I am that Daniel and Ladybird have her, I want to say her name out loud, I want to chant it. I long to meet her again, and this time pay attention to her three dimensions instead of wanting her to pay attention to mine.

What I didn't see for all of our years together was how Daniel took care of me. Setting up my own apartment exposed these cracks in my memory. It had been Daniel scouring thrift stores for art and hanging it on our walls, getting the lighting in our homes to just the right honey glow, and selecting the perfect record to put on the turntable in the mornings. He grew all of our plants—reaped, sowed, watered, and harvested them, bringing me their fruits. He was also in the corners with Rufus at night. He's the one who noticed the drink rings on the windowsill at the cabin. He dressed himself like a demon on Halloween, too.

My confirmation bias led me to selective evidence. He tried so many times to end it, but I refused to part. Each time he cheated he was trying to make it my decision because I wasn't listening to his. I don't subscribe to the method, but now I see the reason.

He was a nurturer too, a father to all, but mostly to me. I was his longest project, the one he cared for the most tenderly and consciously. He was relentless in his efforts to make me laugh—he absolutely lived for it. He's the one who gave me my giggle, so it was his to take back.

We were both trying so hard to take care of each other without consulting the other and eventually exhausted ourselves. Now I see he and Georgina knew how to take care of each other right away. Now my sinuses are clear.

I can't see the Empire State Building anymore—the quickly-built and monstrous high-rises at the waterfront obstruct my view. But I don't worry about it now—I know it's still there. Sometimes on overcast nights I can see its lights reflected in the fog looking back at me like a pair of omniscient eyes. Tonight they're the same shade of green as mine.

Ackowledgements

Thank you:

My first readers Hurley Winkler, Chelsea Hodson, and Giancarlo DiTrapano. Your insight, care, guidance, and enthusiasm were instrumental to shaping this story and emboldening me to continue writing. Thank you to my cohort at the Mors Tua Vita Mea workshop, the birthplace of this book: Hurley Winkler, Mila Jaroniec, Sophie Frost, and Ivan Solis (kind of), and to Giuseppe Avalone for putting up with us.

My publisher D.T. Robbins and *Rejection Letters*. You made this all joy, no burdens. I'm so glad we got to do this together. Thank you Bryce Woodcock for your keen eye and copy edits.

Autofocus and *Joyland* for publishing excerpts of this book. Thank you to Wendy C. Ortiz for selecting and editing much of the Big Sur portion, published in *Joyland*.

Michael Wheaton and Shelby Hinte for being early champions of this manuscript.

To so many beloved buddies for your encouragement and friendship: Marcella Gillis, Meg Stapleton Smith, Benjamin Gibbard, Nicholas Harmer, Allie Rowbottom, Bud Smith, Gia Pisto, Catharine Stuart, Sequoia Chappellet-Volpini, Stefanie Humphries, Sara Winkleblack Elley, Jay Chen, Jessica Rainey, Katie Ly, Claire Taylor, Morgan Cline, Hari Berrier, Ruganzu Howard, Amanda Price, Angela Taylor, James Levy, Elizabeth Gramm, Julia Triplett, Scott Mitchell, Grace Krilanovich, Rufus, and Ladybird.

To my family for your immense love and support: Dana Kent, Bill Monning, Laura Kent-Monning, Kevin Smith, my nieces and nephew who are not allowed to read this until they're 18, Amy Kent, Steve Daggett, Will and Colin Kent-Daggett, Bob Senkfor, Lisa Kent, and Joe Viviano.

In loving memory of Grandma Connie Kent, Aunt Barbie Monning, Giancarlo DiTrapano, Gauraa Shekhar, Joshua Bell, Mark Lanegan, Lynn Shelton, and Ralph "rj" Johnson.

Lexi Kent-Monning is an alumna of the Tyrant Books workshop Mors Tua Vita Mea in Sezze Romano, Italy. Her work has been published in XRAY, Joyland, Tilted House Review, Neutral Spaces, Little Engines, Words and Sports Quarterly, and elsewhere. A native Californian, she now lives in Brooklyn, NY. This is her first book.

www.ingramcontent.com/pod-product-compliance
Lightning Source LLC
Chambersburg PA
CBHW020336160726
47992CB00004B/1867